The Christmas Stories of L

Many great writers are defined and remembered by one pi
culture and continues to be enjoyed by every generation si
it was the brilliant book, Little Women.

Louisa May Alcott

She was born in 1832, in Germantown, Pennsylvania, into an educationally progressive but poor family who were Transcendentalists. She received part of her lessons from distinguished family friends such as Henry David Thoreau, Ralph Waldo Emerson and Nathaniel Hawthorne. These influences on the young Louisa together with her early working life as seamstress, teacher, governess, domestic helper provided much of the material for her later novels.

During the Civil War she worked as a nurse. The letters she wrote home from Georgetown DC were later published and brought sufficient recognition to continue writing not only her passionate novels under the nom de plume A.M. Barnard but also her beloved children's stories.

However, by 1868 she received greater success with critics and audiences with the publication of the first part of the semi autobiographical, Little Women, and despite ill health continued to write until her death at the age of 55.

Alcott was also a poet and a short story writer and here we have gathered together some of those Christmas stories which present her in a very different light and showcase a breadth of talent and experience that still delights to this very day

Index Of Stories

Merry Christmas
In the rush of early morning,
When the red burns through the gray,

And the wintry world lies waiting
For the glory of the day,
Then we hear a fitful rustling
Just without upon the stair,
See two small white phantoms coming,
Catch the gleam of sunny hair.

Are they Christmas fairies stealing
Rows of little socks to fill?
Are they angels floating hither
With their message of good-will?
What sweet spell are these elves weaving,
As like larks they chirp and sing?
Are these palms of peace from heaven
That these lovely spirits bring?

Rosy feet upon the threshold,
Eager faces peeping through,
With the first red ray of sunshine,
Chanting cherubs come in view:
Mistletoe and gleaming holly,
Symbols of a blessed day,
In their chubby hands they carry,
Streaming all along the way.

Well we know them, never weary
Of this innocent surprise;
Waiting, watching, listening always
With full hearts and tender eyes,
While our little household angels,
White and golden in the sun,
Greet us with the sweet old welcome,
"Merry Christmas, every one!"

A Christmas Dream, and How it Came True

"I'm so tired of Christmas I wish there never would be another one!" exclaimed a discontented-looking little girl, as she sat idly watching her mother arrange a pile of gifts two days before they were to be given.

"Why, Effie, what a dreadful thing to say! You are as bad as old Scrooge; and I'm afraid something will happen to you, as it did to him, if you don't care for dear Christmas," answered mamma, almost dropping the silver horn she was filling with delicious candies.

"Who was Scrooge? What happened to him?" asked Effie, with a glimmer of interest in her listless face, as she picked out the sourest lemon-drop she could find; for nothing sweet suited her just then.

"He was one of Dickens's best people, and you can read the charming story some day. He hated Christmas until a strange dream showed him how dear and beautiful it was, and made a better man of him."

"I shall read it; for I like dreams, and have a great many curious ones myself. But they don't keep me from being tired of Christmas," said Effie, poking discontentedly among the sweeties for something worth eating.

"Why are you tired of what should be the happiest time of all the year?" asked mamma, anxiously.

"Perhaps I shouldn't be if I had something new. But it is always the same, and there isn't any more surprise about it. I always find heaps of goodies in my stocking. Don't like some of them, and soon get tired of those I do like. We always have a great dinner, and I eat too much, and feel ill next day. Then there is a Christmas tree somewhere, with a doll on top, or a stupid old Santa Claus, and children dancing and screaming over bonbons and toys that break, and shiny things that are of no use. Really, mamma, I've had so many Christmases all alike that I don't think I can bear another one." And Effie laid herself flat on the sofa, as if the mere idea was too much for her.

Her mother laughed at her despair, but was sorry to see her little girl so discontented, when she had everything to make her happy, and had known but ten Christmas days.

"Suppose we don't give you any presents at all, - how would that suit you?" asked mamma, anxious to please her spoiled child.

"I should like one large and splendid one, and one dear little one, to remember some very nice person by," said Effie, who was a fanciful little body, full of odd whims and notions, which her friends loved to gratify, regardless of time, trouble, or money; for she was the last of three little girls, and very dear to all the family.

"Well, my darling, I will see what I can do to please you, and not say a word until all is ready. If I could only get a new idea to start with!" And mamma went on tying up her pretty bundles with a thoughtful face, while Effie strolled to the window to watch the rain that kept her in-doors and made her dismal.

"Seems to me poor children have better times than rich ones. I can't go out, and there is a girl about my age splashing along, without any maid to fuss about rubbers and cloaks and umbrellas and colds. I wish I was a beggar-girl."

"Would you like to be hungry, cold, and ragged, to beg all day, and sleep on an ash-heap at night?" asked mamma, wondering what would come next.

"Cinderella did, and had a nice time in the end. This girl out here has a basket of scraps on her arm, and a big old shawl all round her, and doesn't seem to care a bit, though the water runs out of the toes of her boots. She goes paddling along, laughing at the rain, and eating a cold potato as if it tasted nicer than the chicken and ice-cream I had for dinner. Yes, I do think poor children are happier than rich ones."

"So do I, sometimes. At the Orphan Asylum today I saw two dozen merry little souls who have no parents, no home, and no hope of Christmas beyond a stick of candy or a cake. I wish you had been there to see how happy they were, playing with the old toys some richer children had sent them."

"You may give them all mine; I'm so tired of them I never want to see them again," said Effie, turning from the window to the pretty baby-house full of everything a child's heart could desire.

"I will, and let you begin again with something you will not tire of, if I can only find it." And mamma knit her brows trying to discover some grand surprise for this child who didn't care for Christmas.

Nothing more was said then; and wandering off to the library, Effie found "A Christmas Carol," and curling herself up in the sofa corner, read it all before tea. Some of it she did not understand; but she laughed and cried over many parts of the charming story, and felt better without knowing why.

All the evening she thought of poor Tiny Tim, Mrs. Cratchit with the pudding, and the stout old gentleman who danced so gayly that "his legs twinkled in the air." Presently bedtime arrived.

"Come, now, and toast your feet," said Effie's nurse, "while I do your pretty hair and tell stories."

"I'll have a fairy tale to-night, a very interesting one," commanded Effie, as she put on her blue silk wrapper and little fur-lined slippers to sit before the fire and have her long curls brushed.

So Nursey told her best tales; and when at last the child lay down under her lace curtains, her head was full of a curious jumble of Christmas elves, poor children, snow-storms, sugarplums, and surprises. So it is no wonder that she dreamed all night; and this was the dream, which she never quite forgot.

She found herself sitting on a stone, in the middle of a great field, all alone. The snow was falling fast, a bitter wind whistled by, and night was coming on. She felt hungry, cold, and tired, and did not know where to go nor what to do.

"I wanted to be a beggar-girl, and now I am one; but I don't like it, and wish somebody would come and take care of me. I don't know who I am, and I think I must be lost," thought Effie, with the curious interest one takes in one's self in dreams.

But the more she thought about it, the more bewildered she felt. Faster fell the snow, colder blew the wind, darker grew the night; and poor Effie made up her mind that she was quite forgotten and left to freeze alone. The tears were chilled on her cheeks, her feet felt like icicles, and her heart died within her, so hungry, frightened, and forlorn was she. Laying her head on her knees, she gave herself up for lost, and sat there with the great flakes fast turning her to a little white mound, when suddenly the sound of music reached her, and starting up, she looked and listened with all her eyes and ears.

Far away a dim light shone, and a voice was heard singing. She tried to run toward the welcome glimmer, but could not stir, and stood like a small statue of expectation while the light drew nearer, and the sweet words of the song grew clearer.

From our happy home
Through the world we roam
One week in all the year,
Making winter spring
With the joy we bring,
For Christmas-tide is here.

Now the eastern star

Shines from afar
To light the poorest home;
Hearts warmer grow,
Gifts freely flow,
For Christmas-tide has come.

Now gay trees rise
Before young eyes,
Abloom with tempting cheer;
Blithe voices sing,
And blithe bells ring,
For Christmas-tide is here.

Oh, happy chime,
Oh, blessed time,
That draws us all so near!
"Welcome, dear day,"
All creatures say,
For Christmas-tide is here.

A child's voice sang, a child's hand carried the little candle; and in the circle of soft light it shed, Effie saw a pretty child coming to her through the night and snow. A rosy, smiling creature, wrapped in white fur, with a wreath of green and scarlet holly on its shining hair, the magic candle in one hand, and the other outstretched as if to shower gifts and warmly press all other hands.

Effie forgot to speak as this bright vision came nearer, leaving no trace of footsteps in the snow, only lighting the way with its little candle, and filling the air with the music of its song.

"Dear child, you are lost, and I have come to find you," said the stranger, taking Effie's cold hands in his, with a smile like sunshine, while every holly berry glowed like a little fire.

"Do you know me?" asked Effie, feeling no fear, but a great gladness, at his coming.

"I know all children, and go to find them; for this is my holiday, and I gather them from all parts of the world to be merry with me once a year."

"Are you an angel?" asked Effie, looking for the wings.

"No; I am a Christmas spirit, and live with my mates in a pleasant place, getting ready for our holiday, when we are let out to roam about the world, helping make this a happy time for all who will let us in. Will you come and see how we work?"

"I will go anywhere with you. Don't leave me again," cried Effie, gladly.

"First I will make you comfortable. That is what we love to do. You are cold, and you shall be warm, hungry, and I will feed you; sorrowful, and I will make you gay."

With a wave of his candle all three miracles were wrought, for the snow-flakes turned to a white fur cloak and hood on Effie's head and shoulders, a bowl of hot soup came sailing to her lips, and vanished when she had eagerly drunk the last drop; and suddenly the dismal field changed to a new world so full of wonders that all her troubles were forgotten in a minute.

Bells were ringing so merrily that it was hard to keep from dancing. Green garlands hung on the walls, and every tree was a Christmas tree full of toys, and blazing with candles that never went out.

In one place many little spirits sewed like mad on warm clothes, turning off work faster than any sewing-machine ever invented, and great piles were made ready to be sent to poor people. Other busy creatures packed money into purses, and wrote checks which they sent flying away on the wind, a lovely kind of snow-storm to fall into a world below full of poverty.

Older and graver spirits were looking over piles of little books, in which the records of the past year were kept, telling how different people had spent it, and what sort of gifts they deserved. Some got peace, some disappointment, some remorse and sorrow, some great joy and hope. The rich had generous thoughts sent them; the poor, gratitude and contentment. Children had more love and duty to parents; and parents renewed patience, wisdom, and satisfaction for and in their children. No one was forgotten.

"Please tell me what splendid place this is?" asked Effie, as soon as she could collect her wits after the first look at all these astonishing things.

"This is the Christmas world; and here we work all the year round, never tired of getting ready for the happy day. See, these are the saints just setting off; for some have far to go, and the children must not be disappointed."

As he spoke the spirit pointed to four gates, out of which four great sleighs were just driving, laden with toys, while a jolly old Santa Claus sat in the middle of each, drawing on his mittens and tucking up his wraps for a long cold drive.

"Why, I thought there was only one Santa Claus, and even he was a humbug," cried Effie, astonished at the sight.

"Never give up your faith in the sweet old stones, even after you come to see that they are only the pleasant shadow of a lovely truth."

Just then the sleighs went off with a great jingling of bells and pattering of reindeer hoofs, while all the spirits gave a cheer that was heard in the lower world, where people said, "Hear the stars sing."

"I never will say there isn't any Santa Claus again. Now, show me more."

"You will like to see this place, I think, and may learn something here perhaps"

The spirit smiled as he led the way to a little door, through which Effie peeped into a world of dolls. Baby-houses were in full blast, with dolls of all sorts going on like live people. Waxen ladies sat in their parlors elegantly dressed; black dolls cooked in the kitchens; nurses walked out with the bits of dollies; and the streets were full of tin soldiers marching, wooden horses prancing, express wagons rumbling, and little men hurrying to and fro. Shops were there, and tiny people buying legs of mutton, pounds of tea, mites of clothes, and everything dolls use or wear or want.

But presently she saw that in some ways the dolls improved upon the manners and customs of human beings, and she watched eagerly to learn why they did these things. A fine Paris doll driving in her carriage took up a black worsted Dinah who was hobbling along with a basket of clean clothes, and carried her to her journey's end, as if it were the proper thing to do. Another interesting china lady took off her comfortable red cloak and put it round a poor wooden creature done up in a paper shift, and so badly painted that its face would have sent some babies into fits.

"Seems to me I once knew a rich girl who didn't give her things to poor girls. I wish I could remember who she was, and tell her to be as kind as that china doll," said Effie, much touched at the sweet way the pretty creature wrapped up the poor fright, and then ran off in her little gray gown to buy a shiny fowl stuck on a wooden platter for her invalid mother's dinner.

"We recall these things to people's minds by dreams. I think the girl you speak of won't forget this one." And the spirit smiled, as if he enjoyed some joke which she did not see.

A little bell rang as she looked, and away scampered the children into the red-and-green school-house with the roof that lifted up, so one could see how nicely they sat at their desks with mites of books, or drew on the inch-square blackboards with crumbs of chalk.

"They know their lessons very well, and are as still as mice. We make a great racket at our school, and get bad marks every day. I shall tell the girls they had better mind what they do, or their dolls will be better scholars than they are," said Effie, much impressed, as she peeped in and saw no rod in the hand of the little mistress, who looked up and shook her head at the intruder, as if begging her to go away before the order of the school was disturbed.

Effie retired at once, but could not resist one look in at the window of a fine mansion, where the family were at dinner, the children behaved so well at table, and never grumbled a bit when their mamma said they could not have any more fruit.

"Now, show me something else," she said, as they came again to the low door that led out of Doll-land.

"You have seen how we prepare for Christmas; let me show you where we love best to send our good and happy gifts," answered the spirit, giving her his hand again.

"I know. I've seen ever so many," began Effie, thinking of her own Christmases.

"No, you have never seen what I will show you. Come away, and remember what you see to-night."

Like a flash that bright world vanished, and Effie found herself in a part of the city she had never seen before. It was far away from the gayer places, where every store was brilliant with lights and full of pretty things, and every house wore a festival air, while people hurried to and fro with merry greetings. It was down among the dingy streets where the poor lived, and where there was no making ready for Christmas.

Hungry women looked in at the shabby shops, longing to buy meat and bread, but empty pockets forbade. Tipsy men drank up their wages in the bar- rooms; and in many cold dark chambers little children huddled under the thin blankets, trying to forget their misery in sleep.

No nice dinners filled the air with savory smells, no gay trees dropped toys and bonbons into eager hands, no little stockings hung in rows beside the chimney-piece ready to be filled, no happy sounds of music, gay voices, and dancing feet were heard; and there were no signs of Christmas anywhere.

"Don't they have any in this place?" asked Effie, shivering, as she held fast the spirit's hand, following where he led her.

"We come to bring it. Let me show you our best workers." And the spirit pointed to some sweet-faced men and women who came stealing into the poor houses, working such beautiful miracles that Effie could only stand and watch.

Some slipped money into the empty pockets, and sent the happy mothers to buy all the comforts they needed; others led the drunken men out of temptation, and took them home to find safer pleasures there. Fires were kindled on cold hearths, tables spread as if by magic, and warm clothes wrapped round shivering limbs. Flowers suddenly bloomed in the chambers of the sick; old people found themselves remembered; sad hearts were consoled by a tender word, and wicked ones softened by the story of Him who forgave all sin.

But the sweetest work was for the children; and Effie held her breath to watch these human fairies hang up and fill the little stockings without which a child's Christmas is not perfect, putting in things that once she would have thought very humble presents, but which now seemed beautiful and precious because these poor babies had nothing.

"That is so beautiful! I wish I could make merry Christmases as these good people do, and be loved and thanked as they are," said Effie, softly, as she watched the busy men and women do their work and steal away without thinking of any reward but their own satisfaction.

"You can if you will. I have shown you the way. Try it, and see how happy your own holiday will be hereafter."

As he spoke, the spirit seemed to put his arms about her, and vanished with a kiss.

"Oh, stay and show me more!" cried Effie, trying to hold him fast.

"Darling, wake up, and tell me why you are smiling in your sleep," said a voice in her ear; and opening her eyes, there was mamma bending over her, and morning sunshine streaming into the room.

"Are they all gone? Did you hear the bells? Wasn't it splendid?" she asked, rubbing her eyes, and looking about her for the pretty child who was so real and sweet.

"You have been dreaming at a great rate, - talking in your sleep, laughing, and clapping your hands as if you were cheering some one. Tell me what was so splendid," said mamma, smoothing the tumbled hair and lifting up the sleepy head.

Then, while she was being dressed, Effie told her dream, and Nursey thought it very wonderful; but mamma smiled to see how curiously things the child had thought, read, heard, and seen through the day were mixed up in her sleep.

"The spirit said I could work lovely miracles if I tried; but I don't know how to begin, for I have no magic candle to make feasts appear, and light up groves of Christmas trees, as he did," said Effie, sorrowfully.

"Yes, you have. We will do it! we will do it!" And clapping her hands, mamma suddenly began to dance all over the room as if she had lost her wits.

"How? how? You must tell me, mamma," cried Effie, dancing after her, and ready to believe anything possible when she remembered the adventures of the past night.

"I've got it! I've got it! the new idea. A splendid one, if I can only carry it out!" And mamma waltzed the little girl round till her curls flew wildly in the air, while Nursey laughed as if she would die.

"Tell me! tell me!" shrieked Effie. "No, no; it is a surprise, a grand surprise for Christmas day!" sung mamma, evidently charmed with her happy thought. "Now, come to breakfast; for we must work like bees if we want to play spirits tomorrow. You and Nursey will go out shopping, and get heaps of things, while I arrange matters behind the scenes."

They were running downstairs as mamma spoke, and Effie called out breathlessly, "It won't be a surprise; for I know you are going to ask some poor children here, and have a tree or something. It won't be like my dream; for they had ever so many trees, and more children than we can find anywhere."

"There will be no tree, no party, no dinner, in this house at all, and no presents for you. Won't that be a surprise?" And mamma laughed at Effie's bewildered face.

"Do it. I shall like it, I think; and I won't ask any questions, so it will all burst upon me when the time comes," she said; and she ate her breakfast thoughtfully, for this really would be a new sort of Christmas.

All that morning Effie trotted after Nursey in and out of shops, buying dozens of barking dogs, woolly lambs, and squeaking birds; tiny tea-sets, gay picture-books, mittens and hoods, dolls and candy. Parcel after parcel was sent home; but when Effie returned she saw no trace of them, though she peeped everywhere. Nursey chuckled, but wouldn't give a hint, and went out again in the afternoon with a long list of more things to buy; while Effie wandered forlornly about the house, missing the usual merry stir that went before the Christmas dinner and the evening fun.

As for mamma, she was quite invisible all day, and came in at night so tired that she could only lie on the sofa to rest, smiling as if some very pleasant thought made her happy in spite of weariness.

"Is the surprise going on all right?" asked Effie, anxiously; for it seemed an immense time to wait till another evening came.

"Beautifully! better than I expected; for several of my good friends are helping, or I couldn't have done it as I wish. I know you will like it, dear, and long remember this new way of making Christmas merry."

Mamma gave her a very tender kiss, and Effie went to bed.

The next day was a very strange one; for when she woke there was no stocking to examine, no pile of gifts under her napkin, no one said "Merry Christmas!" to her, and the dinner was just as usual to her. Mamma vanished again, and Nursey kept wiping her eyes and saying: "The dear things! It's the prettiest idea I ever heard of. No one but your blessed ma could have done it."

"Do stop, Nursey, or I shall go crazy because I don't know the secret!" cried Effie, more than once; and she kept her eye on the clock, for at seven in the evening the surprise was to come off.

The longed-for hour arrived at last, and the child was too excited to ask questions when Nurse put on her cloak and hood, led her to the carriage, and they drove away, leaving their house the one dark and silent one in the row.

"I feel like the girls in the fairy tales who are led off to strange places and see fine things," said Effie, in a whisper, as they jingled through the gay streets.

"Ah, my deary, it is like a fairy tale, I do assure you, and you will see finer things than most children will tonight. Steady, now, and do just as I tell you, and don't say one word whatever you see," answered Nursey, quite quivering with excitement as she patted a large box in her lap, and nodded and laughed with twinkling eyes.

They drove into a dark yard, and Effie was led through a back door to a little room, where Nurse coolly proceeded to take off not only her cloak and hood, but her dress and shoes also. Effie stared and bit her lips, but kept still until out of the box came a little white fur coat and boots, a wreath of holly leaves and berries, and a candle with a frill of gold paper round it. A long "Oh!" escaped her then; and when she was dressed and saw herself in the glass, she started back, exclaiming, "Why, Nursey, I look like the spirit in my dream!"

"So you do; and that's the part you are to play, my pretty! Now whist, while I blind your eyes and put you in your place."

"Shall I be afraid?" whispered Effie, full of wonder; for as they went out she heard the sound of many voices, the tramp of many feet, and, in spite of the bandage, was sure a great light shone upon her when she stopped.

"You needn't be; I shall stand close by, and your ma will be there."

After the handkerchief was tied about her eyes, Nurse led Effie up some steps, and placed her on a high platform, where something like leaves touched her head, and the soft snap of lamps seemed to fill the air.

Music began as soon as Nurse clapped her hands, the voices outside sounded nearer, and the tramp was evidently coming up the stairs.

"Now, my precious, look and see how you and your dear ma have made a merry Christmas for them that needed it!"

Off went the bandage; and for a minute Effie really did think she was asleep again, for she actually stood in "a grove of Christmas trees," all gay and shining as in her vision. Twelve on a side, in two rows down the room, stood the little pines, each on its low table; and behind Effie a taller one rose to the roof, hung with wreaths of popcorn, apples, oranges, horns of candy, and cakes of all sorts, from sugary hearts to gingerbread Jumbos. On the smaller trees she saw many of her own discarded toys and those Nursey bought, as well as heaps that seemed to have rained down straight from that delightful Christmas country where she felt as if she was again.

"How splendid! Who is it for? What is that noise? Where is mamma?" cried Effie, pale with pleasure and surprise, as she stood looking down the brilliant little street from her high place.

Before Nurse could answer, the doors at the lower end flew open, and in marched twenty-four little blue-gowned orphan girls, singing sweetly, until amazement changed the song to cries of joy and wonder as the shining spectacle appeared. While they stood staring with round eyes at the wilderness of pretty things about them, mamma stepped up beside Effie, and holding her hand fast to give her courage, told the story of the dream in a few simple words, ending in this way: -

"So my little girl wanted to be a Christmas spirit too, and make this a happy day for those who had not as many pleasures and comforts as she has. She likes surprises, and we planned this for you all. She shall play the good fairy, and give each of you something from this tree, after which every one will find her own name on a small tree, and can go to enjoy it in her own way. March by, my dears, and let us fill your hands."

Nobody told them to do it, but all the hands were clapped heartily before a single child stirred; then one by one they came to look up wonderingly at the pretty giver of the feast as she leaned down to offer them great yellow oranges, red apples, bunches of grapes, bonbons, and cakes, till all were gone, and a double row of smiling faces turned toward her as the children filed back to their places in the orderly way they had been taught.

Then each was led to her own tree by the good ladies who had helped mamma with all their hearts; and the happy hubbub that arose would have satisfied even Santa Claus himself, shrieks of joy, dances of delight, laughter and tears (for some tender little things could not bear so much pleasure at once, and sobbed with mouths full of candy and hands full of toys). How they ran to show one another the new treasures! how they peeped and tasted, pulled and pinched, until the air was full of queer noises, the floor covered with papers, and the little trees left bare of all but candles!

"I don't think heaven can be any gooder than this," sighed one small girl, as she looked about her in a blissful maze, holding her full apron with one hand, while she luxuriously carried sugar-plums to her mouth with the other.

"Is that a truly angel up there?" asked another, fascinated by the little white figure with the wreath on its shining hair, who in some mysterious way had been the cause of all this merry-making.

"I wish I dared to go and kiss her for this splendid party," said a lame child, leaning on her crutch, as she stood near the steps, wondering how it seemed to sit in a mother's lap, as Effie was doing, while she watched the happy scene before her.

Effie heard her, and remembering Tiny Tim, ran down and put her arms about the pale child, kissing the wistful face, as she said sweetly, "You may; but mamma deserves the thanks. She did it all; I only dreamed about it."

Lame Katy felt as if "a truly angel" was embracing her, and could only stammer out her thanks, while the other children ran to see the pretty spirit, and touch her soft dress, until she stood in a crowd of blue gowns laughing as they held up their gifts for her to see and admire.

Mamma leaned down and whispered one word to the older girls; and suddenly they all took hands to dance round Effie, singing as they skipped.

It was a pretty sight, and the ladies found it hard to break up the happy revel; but it was late for small people, and too much fun is a mistake. So the girls fell into line, and marched before Effie and mamma again, to say goodnight with such grateful little faces that the eyes of those who looked grew dim with tears. Mamma kissed every one; and many a hungry childish heart felt as if the touch of those tender lips was their best gift. Effie shook so many small hands that her own tingled; and when Katy came she pressed a small doll into Effie's hand, whispering, "You didn't have a single present, and we had lots. Do keep that; it's the prettiest thing I got."

"I will," answered Effie, and held it fast until the last smiling face was gone, the surprise all over, and she safe in her own bed, too tired and happy for anything but sleep.

"Mamma, it was a beautiful surprise, and I thank you so much! I don't see how you did it; but I like it best of all the Christmases I ever had, and mean to make one every year. I had my splendid big present, and here is the dear little one to keep for love of poor Katy; so even that part of my wish came true."

And Effie fell asleep with a happy smile on her lips, her one humble gift still in her hand, and a new love for Christmas in her heart that never changed through a long life spent in doing good.

A Country Christmas

"A handful of good life is worth a bushel of learning."

"Dear Emily, I have a brilliant idea, and at once hasten to share it with you. Three weeks ago I came up here to the wilds of Vermont to visit my old aunt, also to get a little quiet and distance in which to survey certain new prospects which have opened before me, and to decide whether I will marry a millionaire and become a queen of society, or remain 'the charming Miss Vaughan' and wait till the conquering hero comes.

"Aunt Plumy begs me to stay over Christmas, and I have consented, as I always dread the formal dinner with which my guardian celebrates the day.

"My brilliant idea is this. I'm going to make it a real old-fashioned frolic, and won't you come and help me? You will enjoy it immensely I am sure, for Aunt is a character. Cousin Saul worth seeing, and Ruth a far prettier girl than any of the city rose-buds coming out this season. Bring Leonard Randal along with you to take notes for his new books; then it will be fresher and truer than the last, clever as it was.

"The air is delicious up here, society amusing, this old farmhouse full of treasures, and your bosom friend pining to embrace you. Just telegraph yes or no, and we will expect you on Tuesday.

"Ever yours,

"SOPHIE VAUGHAN."

"They will both come, for they are as tired of city life and as fond of change as I am," said the writer of the above, as she folded her letter and went to get it posted without delay.

Aunt Plumy was in the great kitchen making pies; a jolly old soul, with a face as ruddy as a winter apple, a cheery voice, and the kindest heart that ever beat under a gingham gown. Pretty Ruth was chopping the mince, and singing so gaily as she worked that the four-and-twenty immortal blackbirds could not have put more music into a pie than she did. Saul was piling wood into the big oven, and Sophie paused a moment on the threshold to look at him, for she always enjoyed the sight of this stalwart cousin, whom she likened to a Norse viking, with his fair hair and beard, keen blue eyes, and six feet of manly height, with shoulders that looked broad and strong enough to bear any burden.

His back was toward her, but he saw her first, and turned his flushed face to meet her, with the sudden lighting up it always showed when she approached.

"I've done it, Aunt; and now I want Saul to post the letter, so we can get a speedy answer."

"Just as soon as I can hitch up, cousin;" and Saul pitched in his last log, looking ready to put a girdle round the earth in less than forty minutes.

"Well, dear, I ain't the least mite of objection, as long as it pleases you. I guess we can stan' it ef your city folks can. I presume to say things will look kind of sing'lar to 'em, but I s'pose that's what they come for. Idle folks do dreadful queer things to amuse 'em;" and Aunt Plumy leaned on the rolling-pin to smile and nod with a shrewd twinkle of her eye, as if she enjoyed the prospect as much as Sophie did.

"I shall be afraid of 'em, but I'll try not to make you ashamed of me," said Ruth, who loved her charming cousin even more than she admired her.

"No fear of that, dear. They will be the awkward ones, and you must set them at ease by just being your simple selves, and treating them as if they were every-day people. Nell is very nice and jolly when she drops her city ways, as she must here. She will enter into the spirit of the fun at once, and I know you'll all like her. Mr. Randal is rather the worse for too much praise and petting, as successful people are apt to be, so a little plain talk and rough work will do him good. He is a true gentleman in spite of his airs and elegance, and he will take it all in good part, if you treat him like a man and not a lion."

"I'll see to him," said Saul, who had listened with great interest to the latter part of Sophie's speech, evidently suspecting a lover, and enjoying the idea of supplying him with a liberal amount of "plain talk and rough work."

"I'll keep 'em busy if that's what they need, for there will be a sight to do, and we can't get help easy up here. Our darters don't hire out much. Work to home till they marry, and don't go gaddin' 'round gettin' their heads full of foolish notions, and forgettin' all the useful things their mothers taught 'em."

Aunt Plumy glanced at Ruth as she spoke, and a sudden color in the girl's cheeks proved that the words hit certain ambitious fancies of this pretty daughter of the house of Basset.

"They shall do their parts and not be a trouble; I'll see to that, for you certainly are the dearest aunt in the world to let me take possession of you and yours in this way," cried Sophie, embracing the old lady with warmth.

Saul wished the embrace could be returned by proxy, as his mother's hands were too floury to do more than hover affectionately round the delicate face that looked so fresh and young beside her wrinkled one. As it could not be done, he fled temptation and "hitched up" without delay.

The three women laid their heads together in his absence, and Sophie's plan grew apace, for Ruth longed to see a real novelist and a fine lady, and Aunt Plumy, having plans of her own to further, said "Yes, dear," to every suggestion.

Great was the arranging and adorning that went on that day in the old farmhouse, for Sophie wanted her friends to enjoy this taste of country pleasures, and knew just what additions would be indispensable to their comfort; what simple ornaments would be in keeping with the rustic stage on which she meant to play the part of prima donna.

Next day a telegram arrived accepting the invitation, for both the lady and the lion. They would arrive that afternoon, as little preparation was needed for this impromptu journey, the novelty of which was its chief charm to these blase people.

Saul wanted to get out the double sleigh and span, for he prided himself on his horses, and a fall of snow came most opportunely to beautify the landscape and add a new pleasure to Christmas festivities.

But Sophie declared that the old yellow sleigh, with Punch, the farm-horse, must be used, as she wished everything to be in keeping; and Saul obeyed, thinking he had never seen anything prettier than his cousin when she appeared in his mother's old-fashioned camlet cloak and blue silk pumpkin hood. He looked remarkably well himself in his fur coat, with hair and beard brushed till they shone like spun gold, a fresh color in his cheek, and the sparkle of amusement in his eyes, while excitement gave his usually grave face the animation it needed to be handsome.

Away they jogged in the creaking old sleigh, leaving Ruth to make herself pretty, with a fluttering heart, and Aunt Plumy to dish up a late dinner fit to tempt the most fastidious appetite.

"She has not come for us, and there is not even a stage to take us up. There must be some mistake," said Emily Herrick, as she looked about the shabby little station where they were set down.

"That is the never-to-be-forgotten face of our fair friend, but the bonnet of her grandmother, if my eyes do not deceive me," answered Randal, turning to survey the couple approaching in the rear.

"Sophie Vaughan, what do you mean by making such a guy of yourself?" exclaimed Emily, as she kissed the smiling face in the hood and stared at the quaint cloak.

"I'm dressed for my part, and I intend to keep it up. This is our host, my cousin, Saul Basset. Come to the sleigh at once, he will see to your luggage," said Sophie, painfully conscious of the antiquity of her array as her eyes rested on Emily's pretty hat and mantle, and the masculine elegance of Randal's wraps.

They were hardly tucked in when Saul appeared with a valise in one hand and a large trunk on his shoulder, swinging both on to a wood-sled that stood near by as easily as if they had been hand-bags.

"That is your hero, is it? Well, he looks it, calm and comely, taciturn and tall," said Emily, in a tone of approbation.

"He should have been named Samson or Goliath; though I believe it was the small man who slung things about and turned out the hero in the end," added Randal, surveying the performance with interest and a touch of envy, for much pen work had made his own hands as delicate as a woman's.

"Saul doesn't live in a glass house, so stones won't hurt him. Remember sarcasm is forbidden and sincerity the order of the day. You are country folks now, and it will do you good to try their simple, honest ways for a few days."

Sophie had no time to say more, for Saul came up and drove off with the brief remark that the baggage would "be along right away."

Being hungry, cold and tired, the guests were rather silent during the short drive, but Aunt Plumy's hospitable welcome, and the savory fumes of the dinner awaiting them, thawed the ice and won their hearts at once.

"Isn't it nice? Aren't you glad you came?" asked Sophie, as she led her friends into the parlor, which she had redeemed from its primness by putting bright chintz curtains to the windows, hemlock boughs over the old portraits, a china bowl of flowers on the table, and a splendid fire on the wide hearth.

"It is perfectly jolly, and this is the way I begin to enjoy myself," answered Emily, sitting down upon the home-made rug, whose red flannel roses bloomed in a blue list basket.

"If I may add a little smoke to your glorious fire, it will be quite perfect. Won't Samson join me?" asked Randal, waiting for permission, cigar-case in hand.

"He has no small vices, but you may indulge yours," answered Sophie, from the depths of a grandmotherly chair.

Emily glanced up at her friend as if she caught a new tone in her voice, then turned to the fire again with a wise little nod, as if confiding some secret to the reflection of herself in the bright brass andiron.

"His Delilah does not take this form. I wait with interest to discover if he has one. What a daisy the sister is. Does she ever speak?" asked Randal, trying to lounge on the haircloth sofa, where he was slipping uncomfortably about.

"Oh yes, and sings like a bird. You shall hear her when she gets over her shyness. But no trifling, mind you, for it is a jealously guarded daisy and not to be picked by any idle hand," said Sophie warningly, as she recalled Ruth's blushes and Randal's compliments at dinner.

"I should expect to be annihilated by the big brother if I attempted any but the 'sincerest' admiration and respect. Have no fears on that score, but tell us what is to follow this superb dinner. An apple bee, spinning match, husking party, or primitive pastime of some sort, I have no doubt."

"As you are new to our ways I am going to let you rest this evening. We will sit about the fire and tell stories. Aunt is a master hand at that, and Saul has reminiscences of the war that are well worth hearing if we can only get him to tell them."

"Ah, he was there, was he?"

"Yes, all through it, and is Major Basset, though he likes his plain name best. He fought splendidly and had several wounds, though only a mere boy when he earned his scars and bars. I'm very proud of him for that," and Sophie looked so as she glanced at the photograph of a stripling in uniform set in the place of honor on the high mantel-piece.

"We must stir him up and hear these martial memories. I want some new incidents, and shall book all I can get, if I may."

Here Randal was interrupted by Saul himself, who came in with an armful of wood for the fire.

"Anything more I can do for you, cousin?" he asked, surveying the scene with a rather wistful look.

"Only come and sit with us and talk over war times with Mr. Randal."

"When I've foddered the cattle and done my chores I'd be pleased to. What regiment were you in?" asked Saul, looking down from his lofty height upon the slender gentleman, who answered briefly,

"In none. I was abroad at the time."

"Sick?"

"No, busy with a novel."

"Took four years to write it?"

"I was obliged to travel and study before I could finish it. These things take more time to work up than outsiders would believe."

"Seems to me our war was a finer story than any you could find in Europe, and the best way to study it would be to fight it out. If you want heroes and heroines you'd have found plenty of 'em there."

"I have no doubt of it, and shall be glad to atone for my seeming neglect of them by hearing about your own exploits. Major."

Randal hoped to turn the conversation gracefully, but Saul was not to be caught, and left the room, saying, with a gleam of fun in his eye,

"I can't stop now; heroes can wait, pigs can't."

The girls laughed at this sudden descent from the sublime to the ridiculous, and Randal joined them, feeling his condescension had not been unobserved.

As if drawn by the merry sound Aunt Plumy appeared, and being established in the rocking-chair fell to talking as easily as if she had known her guests for years.

"Laugh away, young folks, that's better for digestion than any of the messes people use. Are you troubled with dyspepsy, dear? You didn't seem to take your vittles very hearty, so I mistrusted you was delicate," she said, looking at Emily, whose pale cheeks and weary eyes told the story of late hours and a gay life.

"I haven't eaten so much for years, I assure you, Mrs. Basset; but it was impossible to taste all your good things. I am not dyspeptic, thank you, but a little seedy and tired, for I've been working rather hard lately."

"Be you a teacher? or have you a 'perfessun,' as they call a trade nowadays?" asked the old lady in a tone of kindly interest, which prevented a laugh at the idea of Emily's being anything but a beauty and a belle. The others kept their countenances with difficulty, and she answered demurely,

"I have no trade as yet, but I dare say I should be happier if I had."

"Not a doubt on't, my dear."

"What would you recommend, ma'am?"

"I should say dressmakin' was rather in your line, ain't it? Your clothes is dreadful tasty, and do you credit if you made 'em yourself." and Aunt Plumy surveyed with feminine interest the simple elegance of the travelling dress which was the masterpiece of a French modiste.

"No, ma'am, I don't make my own things, I'm too lazy. It takes so much time and trouble to select them that I have only strength left to wear them."

"Housekeepin' used to be the favorite perfessun in my day. It ain't fashionable now, but it needs a sight of trainin' to be perfect in all that's required, and I've an idee it would be a sight healthier and usefuller than the paintin' and music and fancy work young women do nowadays."

"But every one wants some beauty in their lives, and each one has a different sphere to fill, if one can only find it."

"'Pears to me there's no call for so much art when nater is full of beauty for them that can see and love it. As for 'spears' and so on, I've a notion if each of us did up our own little chores smart and thorough we needn't go wanderin' round to set the world to rights. That's the Lord's job, and I presume to say He can do it without any advice of ourn."

Something in the homely but true words seemed to rebuke the three listeners for wasted lives, and for a moment there was no sound but the crackle of the fire, the brisk click of the old lady's knitting needles, and Ruth's voice singing overhead as she made ready to join the party below.

"To judge by that sweet sound you have done one of your 'chores' very beautifully, Mrs. Basset, and in spite of the follies of our day, succeeded in keeping one girl healthy, happy and unspoiled," said Emily, looking up into the peaceful old face with her own lovely one full of respect and envy.

"I do hope so, for she's my ewe lamb, the last of four dear little girls; all the rest are in the burying ground 'side of father. I don't expect to keep her long, and don't ought to regret when I lose her, for Saul is the best of sons; but daughters is more to mothers somehow, and I always yearn over girls that is left without a broodin' wing to keep 'em safe and warm in this world of tribulation."

Aunt Plumy laid her hand on Sophie's head as she spoke, with such a motherly look that both girls drew nearer, and Randal resolved to put her in a book without delay.

Presently Saul returned with little Ruth hanging on his arm and shyly nestling near him as he took the three-cornered leathern chair in the chimney nook, while she sat on a stool close by.

"Now the circle is complete and the picture perfect. Don't light the lamps yet, please, but talk away and let me make a mental study of you. I seldom find so charming a scene to paint," said Randal, beginning to enjoy himself immensely, with a true artist's taste for novelty and effect.

"Tell us about your book, for we have been reading it as it comes out in the magazine, and are much exercised about how it's going to end," began Saul, gallantly throwing himself into the breach, for a momentary embarrassment fell upon the women at the idea of sitting for their portraits before they were ready.

"Do you really read my poor serial up here, and do me the honor to like it?" asked the novelist, both flattered and amused, for his work was of the aesthetic sort, microscopic studies of character, and careful pictures of modern life.

"Sakes alive, why shouldn't we?" cried Aunt Plumy. "We have some eddication, though we ain't very genteel. We've got a town libry, kep up by the women mostly, with fairs and tea parties and so on. We have all the magazines reg'lar, and Saul reads out the pieces while Ruth sews and I knit, my eyes bein' poor. Our winter is long and evenins would be kinder lonesome if we didn't have novils and newspapers to cheer 'em up."

"I am very glad I can help to beguile them for you. Now tell me what you honestly think of my work? Criticism is always valuable, and I should really like yours, Mrs. Basset," said Randal, wondering what the good woman would make of the delicate analysis and worldly wisdom on which he prided himself.

Short work, as Aunt Plumy soon showed him, for she rather enjoyed freeing her mind at all times, and decidedly resented the insinuation that country folk could not appreciate light literature as well as city people.

"I ain't no great of a jedge about anything but nat'ralness of books, and it really does seem as if some of your men and women was dreadful uncomfortable creaters. 'Pears to me it ain't wise to be always pickin' ourselves to pieces and pryin' into things that ought to come gradual by way of experience and the visitations of Providence. Flowers won't blow worth a cent ef you pull 'em open. Better wait and see what they can do alone. I do relish the smart sayins, the odd ways of furrin parts, and the sarcastic slaps at folkses weak spots. But massy knows, we can't live on spice-cake and Charlotte Ruche, and I do feel as if books was more sustainin' ef they was full of every-day people and things, like good bread and butter. Them that goes to the heart and ain't soon forgotten is the kind I hanker for. Mis Terry's books now, and Mis Stowe's, and Dickens's Christmas pieces, them is real sweet and cheerin', to my mind."

As the blunt old lady paused it was evident she had produced a sensation, for Saul smiled at the fire, Ruth looked dismayed at this assault upon one of her idols, and the young ladies were both astonished and amused at the keenness of the new critic who dared express what they had often felt. Randal, however, was quite composed and laughed good-naturedly, though secretly feeling as if a pail of cold water had been poured over him.

"Many thanks, madam; you have discovered my weak point with surprising accuracy. But you see I cannot help 'picking folks to pieces,' as you have expressed it; that is my gift, and it has its attractions, as the sale of my books will testify. People like the 'spice-bread,' and as that is the only sort my oven will bake, I must keep on in order to make my living."

"So rumsellers say, but it ain't a good trade to foller, and I'd chop wood 'fore I'd earn my livin' harmin' my feller man. 'Pears to me I'd let my oven cool a spell, and hunt up some homely, happy folks to write about; folks that don't borrer trouble and go lookin' for holes in their neighbors' coats, but take their lives brave and cheerful; and rememberin' we are all human, have pity on the weak, and try to be as full of mercy, patience and lovin' kindness as Him who made us. That sort of a book would do a heap of good; be real warmin' and strengthening and make them that read it love the man that wrote it, and remember him when he was dead and gone."

"I wish I could!" and Randal meant what he said, for he was as tired of his own style as a watch-maker might be of the magnifying glass through which he strains his eyes all day. He knew that the heart was left out of his work, and that both mind and soul were growing morbid with dwelling on the faulty, absurd and metaphysical phases of life and character. He often threw down his pen and vowed he would write no more; but he loved ease and the books brought money readily; he was accustomed to the stimulant of praise and missed it as the toper misses his wine, so that which had once been a pleasure to himself and others was fast becoming a burden and a disappointment.

The brief pause which followed his involuntary betrayal of discontent was broken by Ruth, who exclaimed, with a girlish enthusiasm that overpowered girlish bashfulness,

"I think all the novels are splendid! I hope you will write hundreds more, and I shall live to read 'em."

"Bravo, my gentle champion! I promise that I will write one more at least, and have a heroine in it whom your mother will both admire and love," answered Randal, surprised to find how grateful he was for the girl's approval, and how rapidly his trained fancy began to paint the background on which he hoped to copy this fresh, human daisy.

Abashed by her involuntary outburst, Ruth tried to efface herself behind Saul's broad shoulder, and he brought the conversation back to its starting-point by saying in a tone of the most sincere interest,

"Speaking of the serial, I am very anxious to know how your hero comes out. He is a fine fellow, and I can't decide whether he is going to spoil his life marrying that silly woman, or do something grand and generous, and not be made a fool of."

"Upon my soul, I don't know myself. It is very hard to find new finales. Can't you suggest something, Major? then I shall not be obliged to leave my story without an end, as people complain I am rather fond of doing."

"Well, no, I don't think I've anything to offer. Seems to me it isn't the sensational exploits that show the hero best, but some great sacrifice quietly made by a common sort of man who is noble without knowing it. I saw a good many such during the war, and often wish I could write them down, for it is surprising how much courage, goodness and real piety is stowed away in common folks ready to show when the right time comes."

"Tell us one of them, and I'll bless you for a hint. No one knows the anguish of an author's spirit when he can't ring down the curtain on an effective tableau," said Randal, with a glance at his friends to ask their aid in eliciting an anecdote or reminiscence.

"Tell about the splendid fellow who held the bridge, like Horatius, till help came up. That was a thrilling story, I assure you," answered Sophie, with an inviting smile.

But Saul would not be his own hero, and said briefly:

"Any man can be brave when the battle-fever is on him, and it only takes a little physical courage to dash ahead." He paused a moment, with his eyes on the snowy landscape without, where twilight was deepening; then, as if constrained by the memory that winter scene evoked, he slowly continued,

"One of the bravest things I ever knew was done by a poor fellow who has been a hero to me ever since, though I only met him that night. It was after one of the big battles of that last winter, and I was knocked over with a broken leg and two or three bullets here and there. Night was coming on, snow falling, and a sharp wind blew over the field where a lot of us lay, dead and alive, waiting for the ambulance to come and pick us up. There was skirmishing going on not far off, and our prospects were rather poor between frost and fire. I was calculating how I'd manage, when I found two poor chaps close by who were worse off, so I braced up and did what I could for them. One had an arm blown away, and kept up a dreadful groaning. The other was shot bad, and bleeding to death for want of help, but never complained. He was nearest, and I liked his pluck, for he spoke cheerful and made me ashamed to growl. Such times make dreadful brutes of men if they haven't something to hold on to, and all three of us were most wild with pain and cold and hunger, for we'd fought all day fasting, when we heard a rumble in the road below, and saw lanterns bobbing round. That meant life to us, and we all tried to holler; two of us were pretty faint, but I managed a good yell, and they heard it.

"'Room for one more. Hard luck, old boys, but we are full and must save the worst wounded first. Take a drink, and hold on till we come back,' says one of them with the stretcher.

"'Here's the one to go,' I says, pointin' out my man, for I saw by the light that he was hard hit.

"'No, that one. He's got more chances than I, or this one; he's young and got a mother; I'll wait,' said the good feller, touchin' my arm, for he 'd heard me mutterin' to myself about this dear old lady. We always want mother when we are down, you know."

Saul's eyes turned to the beloved face with a glance of tenderest affection, and Aunt Plumy answered with a dismal groan at the recollection of his need that night, and her absence.

"Well, to be short, the groaning chap was taken, and my man left. I was mad, but there was no time for talk, and the selfish one went off and left that poor feller to run his one chance. I had my rifle, and guessed I could hobble up to use it if need be; so we settled back to wait without much hope of help, everything being in a muddle. And wait we did till morning, for that ambulance did not come back till next day, when most of us were past needing it.

"I'll never forget that night. I dream it all over again as plain as if it was real. Snow, cold, darkness, hunger, thirst, pain, and all round us cries and cursing growing less and less, till at last only the wind went moaning over that meadow. It was awful! so lonesome, helpless, and seemingly God-forsaken. Hour after hour we lay there side by side under one coat, waiting to be saved or die, for the wind grew strong and we grew weak."

Saul drew a long breath, and held his hands to the fire as if he felt again the sharp suffering of that night.

"And the man?" asked Emily, softly, as if reluctant to break the silence.

"He was a man! In times like that men talk like brothers and show what they are. Lying there, slowly freezing, Joe Cummings told me about his wife and babies, his old folks waiting for him, all depending on him, yet all ready to give him up when he was needed. A plain man, but honest and true, and loving as a woman; I soon saw that as he went on talking, half to me and half to himself, for sometimes he wandered a little toward the end. I've read books, heard sermons, and seen good folks, but nothing ever came so close or did me so much good as seeing this man die. He had one chance and gave it cheerfully. He longed for those he loved, and let 'em go with a good-by they couldn't hear. He suffered all the pains we most shrink from without a murmur, and kept my heart warm while his own was growing cold. It's no use trying to tell that part of it; but I heard prayers that night that meant something, and I saw how faith could hold a soul up when everything was gone but God."

Saul stopped there with a sudden huskiness in his deep voice, and when he went on it was in the tone of one who speaks of a dear friend.

"Joe grew still by and by, and I thought he was asleep, for I felt his breath when I tucked him up, and his hand held on to mine. The cold sort of numbed me, and I dropped off, too weak and stupid to think or feel. I never should have waked up if it hadn't been for Joe. When I came to, it was morning, and I thought I was dead, for all I could see was that great field of white mounds, like graves, and a splendid sky above. Then I looked for Joe, remembering; but he had put my coat back over me, and lay stiff and still under the snow that covered him like a shroud, all except his face. A bit of my cape had blown over it, and when I took it off and the sun shone on his dead face, I declare to you it was so full of heavenly peace I felt as if that common man had been glorified by God's light, and rewarded by God's 'Well done.' That's all."

No one spoke for a moment, while the women wiped their eyes, and Saul dropped his as if to hide something softer than tears.

"It was very noble, very touching. And you? how did you get off at last?" asked Randal, with real admiration and respect in his usually languid face.

"Crawled off," answered Saul, relapsing into his former brevity of speech.

"Why not before, and save yourself all that misery?"

"Couldn't leave Joe."

"Ah, I see; there were two heroes that night."

"Dozens, I've no doubt. Those were times that made heroes of men, and women, too."

"Tell us more;" begged Emily, looking up with an expression none of her admirers ever brought to her face by their softest compliments or wiliest gossip.

"I've done my part. It's Mr. Randal's turn now;" and Saul drew himself out of the ruddy circle of firelight, as if ashamed of the prominent part he was playing.

Sophie and her friend had often heard Randal talk, for he was an accomplished raconteur, but that night he exerted himself, and was unusually brilliant and entertaining, as if upon his mettle. The Bassets were charmed. They sat late and were very merry, for Aunt Plumy got up a little supper for them, and her cider was as exhilarating as champagne. When they parted for the night and Sophie kissed her aunt, Emily did the same, saying heartily,

"It seems as if I'd known you all my life, and this is certainly the most enchanting old place that ever was."

"Glad you like it, dear. But it ain't all fun, as you'll find out to-morrow when you go to work, for Sophie says you must," answered Mrs. Basset, as her guests trooped away, rashly promising to like everything.

They found it difficult to keep their word when they were called at half past six next morning. Their rooms were warm, however, and they managed to scramble down in time for breakfast, guided by the fragrance of coffee and Aunt Plumy's shrill voice singing the good old hymn

"Lord, in the morning Thou shalt hear
My voice ascending high."

An open fire blazed on the hearth, for the cooking was done in the lean-to, and the spacious, sunny kitchen was kept in all its old-fashioned perfection, with the wooden settle in a warm nook, the tall clock behind the door, copper and pewter utensils shining on the dresser, old china in the corner closet and a little spinning wheel rescued from the garret by Sophie to adorn the deep window, full of scarlet geraniums, Christmas roses, and white chrysanthemums.

The young lady, in a checked apron and mob-cap, greeted her friends with a dish of buckwheats in one hand, and a pair of cheeks that proved she had been learning to fry these delectable cakes.

"You do 'keep it up' in earnest, upon my word; and very becoming it is, dear. But won't you ruin your complexion and roughen your hands if you do so much of this new fancy-work?" asked Emily, much amazed at this novel freak.

"I like it, and really believe I've found my proper sphere at last. Domestic life seems so pleasant to me that I feel as if I'd better keep it up for the rest of my life," answered Sophie, making a pretty picture of herself as she cut great slices of brown bread, with the early sunshine touching her happy face.

"The charming Miss Vaughan in the role of a farmer's wife. I find it difficult to imagine, and shrink from the thought of the wide-spread dismay such a fate will produce among her adorers," added Randal, as he basked in the glow of the hospitable fire.

"She might do worse; but come to breakfast and do honor to my handiwork," said Sophie, thinking of her worn-out millionaire, and rather nettled by the satiric smile on Randal's lips.

"What an appetite early rising gives one. I feel equal to almost anything, so let me help wash cups," said Emily, with unusual energy, when the hearty meal was over and Sophie began to pick up the dishes as if it was her usual work.

Ruth went to the window to water the flowers, and Randal followed to make himself agreeable, remembering her defence of him last night. He was used to admiration from feminine eyes, and flattery from soft lips, but found something new and charming in the innocent delight which showed itself at his approach in blushes more eloquent than words, and shy glances from eyes full of hero-worship.

"I hope you are going to spare me a posy for to-morrow night, since I can be fine in no other way to do honor to the dance Miss Sophie proposes for us," he said, leaning in the bay window to look down on the little girl, with the devoted air he usually wore for pretty women.

"Anything you like! I should be so glad to have you wear my flowers. There will be enough for all, and I've nothing else to give to people who have made me as happy as cousin Sophie and you," answered Ruth, half drowning her great calla as she spoke with grateful warmth.

"You must make her happy by accepting the invitation to go home with her which I heard given last night. A peep at the world would do you good, and be a pleasant change, I think."

"Oh, very pleasant! but would it do me good?" and Ruth looked up with sudden seriousness in her blue eyes, as a child questions an elder, eager, yet wistful.

"Why not?" asked Randal, wondering at the hesitation.

"I might grow discontented with things here if I saw splendid houses and fine people. I am very happy now, and it would break my heart to lose that happiness, or ever learn to be ashamed of home."

"But don't you long for more pleasure, new scenes and other friends than these?" asked the man, touched by the little creature's loyalty to the things she knew and loved.

"Very often, but mother says when I'm ready they will come, so I wait and try not to be impatient." But Ruth's eyes looked out over the green leaves as if the longing was very strong within her to see more of the unknown world lying beyond the mountains that hemmed her in.

"It is natural for birds to hop out of the nest, so I shall expect to see you over there before long, and ask you how you enjoy your first flight," said Randal, in a paternal tone that had a curious effect on Ruth.

To his surprise, she laughed, then blushed like one of her own roses, and answered with a demure dignity that was very pretty to see.

"I intend to hop soon, but it won't be a very long flight or very far from mother. She can't spare me, and nobody in the world can fill her place to me."

"Bless the child, does she think I'm going to make love to her," thought Randal, much amused, but quite mistaken. Wiser women had thought so when he assumed the caressing air with which he beguiled them into the little revelations of character he liked to use, as the south wind makes flowers open their hearts to give up their odor, then leaves them to carry it elsewhere, the more welcome for the stolen sweetness.

"Perhaps you are right. The maternal wing is a safe shelter for confiding little souls like you, Miss Ruth. You will be as comfortable here as your flowers in this sunny window," he said, carelessly pinching geranium leaves, and ruffling the roses till the pink petals of the largest fluttered to the floor.

As if she instinctively felt and resented something in the man which his act symbolized, the girl answered quietly, as she went on with her work, "Yes, if the frost does not touch me, or careless people spoil me too soon."

Before Randal could reply Aunt Plumy approached like a maternal hen who sees her chicken in danger.

"Saul is goin' to haul wood after he's done his chores, mebbe you'd like to go along? The view is good, the roads well broke, and the day uncommon fine."

"Thanks; it will be delightful, I dare say," politely responded the lion, with a secret shudder at the idea of a rural promenade at 8 A.M. in the winter.

"Come on, then; we'll feed the stock, and then I'll show you how to yoke oxen," said Saul, with a twinkle in his eye as he led the way, when his new aide had muffled himself up as if for a polar voyage.

"Now, that's too bad of Saul! He did it on purpose, just to please you, Sophie," cried Ruth presently, and the girls ran to the window to behold Randal bravely following his host with a pail of pigs' food in each hand, and an expression of resigned disgust upon his aristocratic face.

"To what base uses may we come," quoted Emily, as they all nodded and smiled upon the victim as he looked back from the barn-yard, where he was clamorously welcomed by his new charges.

"It is rather a shock at first, but it will do him good, and Saul won't be too hard upon him, I'm sure," said Sophie, going back to her work, while Ruth turned her best buds to the sun that they might be ready for a peace-offering to-morrow.

There was a merry clatter in the big kitchen for an hour; then Aunt Plumy and her daughter shut themselves up in the pantry to perform some culinary rites, and the young ladies went to inspect certain antique costumes laid forth in Sophie's room.

"You see, Em, I thought it would be appropriate to the house and season to have an old-fashioned dance. Aunt has quantities of ancient finery stowed away, for great-grandfather Basset was a fine old gentleman and his family lived in state. Take your choice of the crimson, blue or silver-gray damask. Ruth is to wear the worked muslin and quilted white satin skirt, with that coquettish hat."

"Being dark, I'll take the red and trim it up with this fine lace. You must wear the blue and primrose, with the distracting high-heeled shoes. Have you any suits for the men?" asked Emily, throwing herself at once into the all-absorbing matter of costume.

"A claret velvet coat and vest, silk stockings, cocked hat and snuff-box for Randal. Nothing large enough for Saul, so he must wear his uniform. Won't Aunt Plumy be superb in this plum-colored satin and immense cap?"

A delightful morning was spent in adapting the faded finery of the past to the blooming beauty of the present, and time and tongues flew till the toot of a horn called them down to dinner.

The girls were amazed to see Randal come whistling up the road with his trousers tucked into his boots, blue mittens on his hands, and an unusual amount of energy in his whole figure, as he drove the oxen, while Saul laughed at his vain attempts to guide the bewildered beasts.

"It's immense! The view from the hill is well worth seeing, for the snow glorifies the landscape and reminds one of Switzerland. I'm going to make a sketch of it this afternoon; better come and enjoy the delicious freshness, young ladies."

Randal was eating with such an appetite that he did not see the glances the girls exchanged as they promised to go.

"Bring home some more winter-green, I want things to be real nice, and we haven't enough for the kitchen," said Ruth, dimpling with girlish delight as she imagined herself dancing under the green garlands in her grandmother's wedding gown.

It was very lovely on the hill, for far as the eye could reach lay the wintry landscape sparkling with the brief beauty of sunshine on virgin snow. Pines sighed overhead, hardy birds flitted to and fro, and in all the trodden spots rose the little spires of evergreen ready for its Christmas duty. Deeper in the wood sounded the measured ring of axes, the crash of falling trees, while the red shirts of the men added color to the scene, and a fresh wind brought the aromatic breath of newly cloven hemlock and pine.

"How beautiful it is! I never knew before what winter woods were like. Did you, Sophie?" asked Emily, sitting on a stump to enjoy the novel pleasure at her ease.

"I've found out lately; Saul lets me come as often as I like, and this fine air seems to make a new creature of me," answered Sophie, looking about her with sparkling eyes, as if this was a kingdom where she reigned supreme.

"Something is making a new creature of you, that is very evident. I haven't yet discovered whether it is the air or some magic herb among that green stuff you are gathering so diligently;" and Emily laughed to see the color deepen beautifully in her friend's half-averted face.

"Scarlet is the only wear just now, I find. If we are lost like babes in the woods there are plenty of redbreasts to cover us with leaves," and Randal joined Emily's laugh, with a glance at Saul, who had just pulled his coat off.

"You wanted to see this tree go down, so stand from under and I'll show you how it's done," said the farmer, taking up his axe, not unwilling to gratify his guests and display his manly accomplishments at the same time.

It was a fine sight, the stalwart man swinging his axe with magnificent strength and skill, each blow sending a thrill through the stately tree, till its heart was reached and it tottered to its fall. Never pausing for breath Saul shook his yellow mane out of his eyes, and hewed away, while the drops stood on his forehead and his arm ached, as bent on distinguishing himself as if he had been a knight tilting against his rival for his lady's favor.

"I don't know which to admire most, the man or his muscle. One doesn't often see such vigor, size and comeliness in these degenerate days," said Randal, mentally booking the fine figure in the red shirt.

"I think we have discovered a rough diamond. I only wonder if Sophie is going to try and polish it," answered Emily, glancing at her friend, who stood a little apart, watching the rise and fall of the axe as intently as if her fate depended on it.

Down rushed the tree at last, and, leaving them to examine a crow's nest in its branches, Saul went off to his men, as if he found the praises of his prowess rather too much for him.

Randal fell to sketching, the girls to their garland-making, and for a little while the sunny woodland nook was full of lively chat and pleasant laughter, for the air exhilarated them all like wine. Suddenly a man came running from the wood, pale and anxious, saying, as he hastened by for help, "Blasted tree fell on him! Bleed to death before the doctor comes!"

"Who? who?" cried the startled trio.

But the man ran on, with some breathless reply, in which only a name was audible - "Basset."

"The deuce it is!" and Randal dropped his pencil, while the girls sprang up in dismay. Then, with one impulse, they hastened to the distant group, half visible behind the fallen trees and corded wood.

Sophie was there first, and forcing her way through the little crowd of men, saw a red-shirted figure on the ground, crushed and bleeding, and threw herself down beside it with a cry that pierced the hearts of those who heard it.

In the act she saw it was not Saul, and covered her bewildered face as if to hide its joy. A strong arm lifted her, and the familiar voice said cheeringly,

"I'm all right, dear. Poor Bruce is hurt, but we've sent for help. Better go right home and forget all about it."

"Yes, I will, if I can do nothing;" and Sophie meekly returned to her friends who stood outside the circle over which Saul's head towered, assuring them of his safety.

Hoping they had not seen her agitation, she led Emily away, leaving Randal to give what aid he could and bring them news of the poor wood-chopper's state.

Aunt Plumy produced the "camphire" the moment she saw Sophie's pale face, and made her lie down, while the brave old lady trudged briskly off with bandages and brandy to the scene of action. On her return she brought comfortable news of the man, so the little flurry blew over and was forgotten by all but Sophie, who remained pale and quiet all the evening, tying evergreen as if her life depended on it.

"A good night's sleep will set her up. She ain't used to such things, dear child, and needs cossetin'," said Aunt Plumy, purring over her until she was in her bed, with a hot stone at her feet and a bowl of herb tea to quiet her nerves.

An hour later when Emily went up, she peeped in to see if Sophie was sleeping nicely, and was surprised to find the invalid wrapped in a dressing-gown writing busily.

"Last will and testament, or sudden inspiration, dear? How are you? faint or feverish, delirious or in the dumps! Saul looks so anxious, and Mrs. Basset hushes us all up so, I came to bed, leaving Randal to entertain Ruth."

As she spoke Emily saw the papers disappear in a portfolio, and Sophie rose with a yawn.

"I was writing letters, but I'm sleepy now. Quite over my foolish fright, thank you. Go and get your beauty sleep that you may dazzle the natives to-morrow."

"So glad, good night;" and Emily went away, saying to herself, "Something is going on, and I must find out what it is before I leave. Sophie can't blind me."

But Sophie did all the next day, being delightfully gay at the dinner, and devoting herself to the young minister who was invited to meet the distinguished novelist, and evidently being afraid of him, gladly basked in the smiles of his charming neighbor. A dashing sleigh-ride occupied the afternoon, and then great was the fun and excitement over the costumes.

Aunt Plumy laughed till the tears rolled down her cheeks as the girls compressed her into the plum-colored gown with its short waist, leg-of-mutton sleeves, and narrow skirt. But a worked scarf hid all deficiencies, and the towering cap struck awe into the soul of the most frivolous observer.

"Keep an eye on me, girls, for I shall certainly split somewheres or lose my head-piece off when I'm trottin' round. What would my blessed mother say if she could see me rigged out in her best things?" and with a smile and a sigh the old lady departed to look after "the boys," and see that the supper was all right.

Three prettier damsels never tripped down the wide staircase than the brilliant brunette in crimson brocade, the pensive blonde in blue, or the rosy little bride in old muslin and white satin.

A gallant court gentleman met them in the hall with a superb bow, and escorted them to the parlor, where Grandma Basset's ghost was discovered dancing with a modern major in full uniform.

Mutual admiration and many compliments followed, till other ancient ladies and gentlemen arrived in all manner of queer costumes, and the old house seemed to wake from its humdrum quietude to sudden music and merriment, as if a past generation had returned to keep its Christmas there.

The village fiddler soon struck up the good old tunes, and then the strangers saw dancing that filled them with mingled mirth and envy; it was so droll, yet so hearty. The young men, unusually awkward in their grandfathers' knee-breeches, flapping vests, and swallow-tail coats, footed it bravely with the buxom girls who were the prettier for their quaintness, and danced with such vigor that their high combs stood awry, their furbelows waved wildly, and their cheeks were as red as their breast-knots, or hose.

It was impossible to stand still, and one after the other the city folk yielded to the spell, Randal leading off with Ruth, Sophie swept away by Saul, and Emily being taken possession of by a young giant of eighteen, who spun her around with a boyish impetuosity that took her breath away. Even Aunt Plumy was discovered jigging it alone in the pantry, as if the music was too much for her, and the plates and glasses jingled gaily on the shelves in time to Money Musk and Fishers' Hornpipe.

A pause came at last, however, and fans fluttered, heated brows were wiped, jokes were made, lovers exchanged confidences, and every nook and corner held a man and maid carrying on the sweet game which is never out of fashion. There was a glitter of gold lace in the back entry, and a train of blue and primrose shone in the dim light. There was a richer crimson than that of the geraniums in the deep window, and a dainty shoe tapped the bare floor impatiently as the brilliant black eyes looked everywhere for the court gentleman, while their owner listened to the gruff prattle of an enamored boy. But in the upper hall walked a little white ghost as if waiting for some shadowy companion, and when a dark form appeared ran to take its arm, saying, in a tone of soft satisfaction,

"I was so afraid you wouldn't come!"

"Why did you leave me, Ruth?" answered a manly voice in a tone of surprise, though the small hand slipping from the velvet coat-sleeve was replaced as if it was pleasant to feel it there.

A pause, and then the other voice answered demurely,

"Because I was afraid my head would be turned by the fine things you were saying."

"It is impossible to help saying what one feels to such an artless little creature as you are. It does me good to admire anything so fresh and sweet, and won't harm you."

"It might if -"

"If what, my daisy?"

"I believed it," and a laugh seemed to finish the broken sentence better than the words.

"You may, Ruth, for I do sincerely admire the most genuine girl I have seen for a long time. And walking here with you in your bridal white I was just asking myself if I should not be a happier man with a home of my own and a little wife hanging on my arm than drifting about the world as I do now with only myself to care for."

"I know you would!" and Ruth spoke so earnestly that Randal was both touched and startled, fearing he had ventured too far in a mood of unwonted sentiment, born of the romance of the hour and the sweet frankness of his companion.

"Then you don't think it would be rash for some sweet woman to take me in hand and make me happy, since fame is a failure?"

"Oh, no; it would be easy work if she loved you. I know some one, if I only dared to tell her name."

"Upon my soul, this is cool," and Randal looked down, wondering if the audacious lady on his arm could be shy Ruth.

If he had seen the malicious merriment in her eyes he would have been more humiliated still, but they were modestly averted, and the face under the little hat was full of a soft agitation rather dangerous even to a man of the world.

"She is a captivating little creature, but it is too soon for anything but a mild flirtation. I must delay further innocent revelations or I shall do something rash."

While making this excellent resolution Randal had been pressing the hand upon his arm and gently pacing down the dimly lighted hall with the sound of music in his ears, Ruth's sweetest roses in his button-hole, and a loving little girl beside him, as he thought.

"You shall tell me by and by when we are in town. I am sure you will come, and meanwhile don't forget me."

"I am going in the spring, but I shall not be with Sophie," answered Ruth, in a whisper.

"With whom then? I shall long to see you."

"With my husband. I am to be married in May."

"The deuce you are!" escaped Randal, as he stopped short to stare at his companion, sure she was not in earnest.

But she was, for as he looked the sound of steps coming up the back stairs made her whole face flush and brighten with the unmistakable glow of happy love, and she completed Randal's astonishment by running into the arms of the young minister, saying with an irrepressible laugh, "Oh, John, why didn't you come before?"

The court gentleman was all right in a moment, and the coolest of the three as he offered his congratulations and gracefully retired, leaving the lovers to enjoy the tryst he had delayed. But as he went down stairs his brows were knit, and he slapped the broad railing smartly with his cocked hat as if some irritation must find vent in a more energetic way than merely saying, "Confound the little baggage!" under his breath.

Such an amazing supper came from Aunt Plumy's big pantry that the city guests could not eat for laughing at the queer dishes circulating through the rooms, and copiously partaken of by the hearty young folks.

Doughnuts and cheese, pie and pickles, cider and tea, baked beans and custards, cake and cold turkey, bread and butter, plum pudding and French bonbons, Sophie's contribution.

"May I offer you the native delicacies, and share your plate? Both are very good, but the china has run short, and after such vigorous exercise as you have had you must need refreshment. I'm sure I do!" said Randal, bowing before Emily with a great blue platter laden with two doughnuts, two wedges of pumpkin pie and two spoons.

The smile with which she welcomed him, the alacrity with which she made room beside her and seemed to enjoy the supper he brought, was so soothing to his ruffled spirit that he soon began to feel that there is no friend like an old friend, that it would not be difficult to name a sweet woman who would take him in hand and would make him happy if he cared to ask her, and he began to think he would by and by, it was so pleasant to sit in that green corner with waves of crimson brocade flowing over his feet, and a fine face softening beautifully under his eyes.

The supper was not romantic, but the situation was, and Emily found that pie ambrosial food eaten with the man she loved, whose eyes talked more eloquently than the tongue just then busy with a doughnut. Ruth kept away, but glanced at them as she served her company, and her own happy experience helped her to see that all was going well in that quarter. Saul and Sophie emerged from the back entry with shining countenances, but carefully avoided each other for the rest of the evening. No one observed this but Aunt Plumy from the recesses of her pantry, and she folded her hands as if well content, as she murmured fervently over a pan full of crullers, "Bless the dears! Now I can die happy."

Every one thought Sophie's old-fashioned dress immensely becoming, and several of his former men said to Saul with blunt admiration, "Major, you look to-night as you used to after we'd gained a big battle."

"I feel as if I had," answered the splendid Major, with eyes much brighter than his buttons, and a heart under them infinitely prouder than when he was promoted on the field of honor, for his Waterloo was won.

There was more dancing, followed by games, in which Aunt Plumy shone pre-eminent, for the supper was off her mind and she could enjoy herself. There were shouts of merriment as the blithe old lady twirled the platter, hunted the squirrel, and went to Jerusalem like a girl of sixteen; her cap in a ruinous condition, and every seam of the purple dress straining like sails in a gale. It was great fun, but at midnight it came to an end, and the young folks, still bubbling over with innocent jollity, went jingling away along the snowy hills, unanimously pronouncing Mrs. Basset's party the best of the season.

"Never had such a good time in my life!" exclaimed Sophie, as the family stood together in the kitchen where the candles among the wreaths were going out, and the floor was strewn with wrecks of past joy.

"I'm proper glad, dear. Now you all go to bed and lay as late as you like to-morrow. I'm so kinder worked up I couldn't sleep, so Saul and me will put things to rights without a mite of noise to disturb you;" and Aunt Plumy sent them off with a smile that was a benediction, Sophie thought.

"The dear old soul speaks as if midnight was an unheard-of hour for Christians to be up. What would she say if she knew how we seldom go to bed till dawn in the ball season? I'm so wide awake I've half a mind to pack a little. Randal must go at two, he says, and we shall want his escort," said Emily, as the girls laid away their brocades in the press in Sophie's room.

"I'm not going. Aunt can't spare me, and there is nothing to go for yet," answered Sophie, beginning to take the white chrysanthemums out of her pretty hair.

"My dear child, you will die of ennui up here. Very nice for a week or so, but frightful for a winter. We are going to be very gay, and cannot get on without you," cried Emily dismayed at the suggestion.

"You will have to, for I'm not coming. I am very happy here, and so tired of the frivolous life I lead in town, that I have decided to try a better one," and Sophie's mirror reflected a face full of the sweetest content.

"Have you lost your mind? experienced religion? or any other dreadful thing? You always were odd, but this last freak is the strangest of all. What will your guardian say, and the world?" added Emily in the awe-stricken tone of one who stood in fear of the omnipotent Mrs. Grundy.

"Guardy will be glad to be rid of me, and I don't care that for the world," cried Sophie, snapping her fingers with a joyful sort of recklessness which completed Emily's bewilderment.

"But Mr. Hammond? Are you going to throw away millions, lose your chance of making the best match in the city, and driving the girls of our set out of their wits with envy?"

Sophie laughed at her friend's despairing cry, and turning round said quietly,

"I wrote to Mr. Hammond last night, and this evening received my reward for being an honest girl. Saul and I are to be married in the spring when Ruth is."

Emily fell prone upon the bed as if the announcement was too much for her, but was up again in an instant to declare with prophetic solemnity,

"I knew something was going on, but hoped to get you away before you were lost. Sophie, you will repent. Be warned, and forget this sad delusion."

"Too late for that. The pang I suffered yesterday when I thought Saul was dead showed me how well I loved him. To-night he asked me to stay, and no power in the world can part us. Oh! Emily, it is all so sweet, so beautiful, that everything is possible, and I know I shall be happy in this dear old home, full of love and peace and honest hearts. I only hope you may find as true and tender a man to live for as my Saul."

Sophie's face was more eloquent than her fervent words, and Emily beautifully illustrated the inconsistency of her sex by suddenly embracing her friend, with the incoherent exclamation, "I think I have, dear! Your brave Saul is worth a dozen old Hammonds, and I do believe you are right."

It is unnecessary to tell how, as if drawn by the irresistible magic of sympathy, Ruth and her mother crept in one by one to join the midnight conference and add their smiles and tears, tender hopes and proud delight to the joys of that memorable hour. Nor how Saul, unable to sleep, mounted guard below, and meeting Randal prowling down to soothe his nerves with a surreptitious cigar found it impossible to help confiding to his attentive ear the happiness that would break bounds and overflow in unusual eloquence.

Peace fell upon the old house at last, and all slept as if some magic herb had touched their eyelids, bringing blissful dreams and a glad awakening.

"Can't we persuade you to come with us, Miss Sophie?" asked Randal next day, as they made their adieux.

"I'm under orders now, and dare not disobey my superior officer," answered Sophie, handing her Major his driving gloves, with a look which plainly showed that she had joined the great army of devoted women who enlist for life and ask no pay but love.

"I shall depend on being invited to your wedding, then, and yours, too, Miss Ruth," added Randal, shaking hands with "the little baggage," as if he had quite forgiven her mockery and forgotten his own brief lapse into sentiment.

Before she could reply Aunt Plumy said, in a tone of calm conviction, that made them all laugh, and some of them look conscious,

"Spring is a good time for weddin's, and I shouldn't wonder ef there was quite a number."

"Nor I;" and Saul and Sophie smiled at one another as they saw how carefully Randal arranged Emily's wraps.

Then with kisses, thanks and all the good wishes that happy hearts could imagine, the guests drove away, to remember long and gratefully that pleasant country Christmas.

The Abbot's Ghost, Or Maurice Treherne's Temptation (writing as A. M. Barnard)

A Christmas Story

Chapter I

Dramatis Personae

"How goes it, Frank? Down first, as usual."

"The early bird gets the worm, Major."

"Deuced ungallant speech, considering that the lovely Octavia is the worm," and with a significant laugh the major assumed an Englishman's favorite attitude before the fire.

His companion shot a quick glance at him, and an expression of anxiety passed over his face as he replied, with a well-feigned air of indifference, "You are altogether too sharp, Major. I must be on my guard while you are in the house. Any new arrivals? I thought I heard a carriage drive up not long ago."

"It was General Snowdon and his charming wife. Maurice Treherne came while we were out, and I've not seen him yet, poor fellow!"

"Aye, you may well say that; his is a hard case, if what I heard is true. I'm not booked up in the matter, and I should be, lest I make some blunder here, so tell me how things stand, Major. We've a good half hour before dinner. Sir Jasper is never punctual."

"Yes, you've a right to know, if you are going to try your fortune with Octavia."

The major marched through the three drawing rooms to see that no inquisitive servant was eavesdropping, and, finding all deserted, he resumed his place, while young Annon lounged on a couch as he listened with intense interest to the major's story.

"You know it was supposed that old Sir Jasper, being a bachelor, would leave his fortune to his two nephews. But he was an oddity, and as the title must go to young Jasper by right, the old man said Maurice should have the money. He was poor, young Jasper rich, and it seemed but just, though Madame Mère was very angry when she learned how the will was made."

"But Maurice didn't get the fortune. How was that?"

"There was some mystery there which I shall discover in time. All went smoothly till that unlucky yachting trip, when the cousins were wrecked. Maurice saved Jasper's life, and almost lost his own in so doing. I fancy he wishes he had, rather than remain the poor cripple he is. Exposure, exertion, and neglect afterward brought on paralysis of the lower limbs, and there he is, a fine, talented, spirited fellow tied to that cursed chair like a decrepit old man."

"How does he bear it?" asked Annon, as the major shook his gray head, with a traitorous huskiness in his last words.

"Like a philosopher or a hero. He is too proud to show his despair at such a sudden end to all his hopes, too generous to complain, for Jasper is desperately cut up about it, and too brave to be daunted by a misfortune which would drive many a man mad."

"Is it true that Sir Jasper, knowing all this, made a new will and left every cent to his namesake?"

"Yes, and there lies the mystery. Not only did he leave it away from poor Maurice, but so tied it up that Jasper cannot transfer it, and at his death it goes to Octavia."

"The old man must have been demented. What in heaven's name did he mean by leaving Maurice helpless and penniless after all his devotion to Jasper? Had he done anything to offend the old party?"

"No one knows; Maurice hasn't the least idea of the cause of this sudden whim, and the old man would give no reason for it. He died soon after, and the instant Jasper came to the title and estate he brought his cousin home, and treats him like a brother. Jasper is a noble fellow, with all his faults, and this act of justice increases my respect for him," said the major heartily.

"What will Maurice do, now that he can't enter the army as he intended?" asked Annon, who now sat erect, so full of interest was he.

"Marry Octavia, and come to his own, I hope."

"An excellent little arrangement, but Miss Treherne may object," said Annon, rising with sudden kindling of the eye.

"I think not, if no one interferes. Pity, with women, is akin to love, and she pities her cousin in the tenderest fashion. No sister could be more devoted, and as Maurice is a handsome, talented fellow, one can easily foresee the end, if, as I said before, no one interferes to disappoint the poor lad again."

"You espouse his cause, I see, and tell me this that I may stand aside. Thanks for the warning, Major; but as Maurice Treherne is a man of unusual power in many ways, I think we are equally matched, in spite of his misfortune. Nay, if anything, he has the advantage of me, for Miss Treherne pities him, and that is a strong ally for my rival. I'll be as generous as I can, but I'll not stand aside and relinquish the woman I love without a trial first."

With an air of determination Annon faced the major, whose keen eyes had read the truth which he had but newly confessed to himself. Major Royston smiled as he listened, and said briefly, as steps approached, "Do your best. Maurice will win."

"We shall see," returned Annon between his teeth.

Here their host entered, and the subject of course was dropped. But the major's words rankled in the young man's mind, and would have been doubly bitter had he known that their confidential conversation had been overheard. On either side of the great fireplace was a door leading to a suite of rooms which had been old Sir Jasper's. These apartments had been given to Maurice Treherne, and he had just returned from London, whither he had been to consult a certain famous physician. Entering quietly, he had taken possession of his rooms, and having rested and dressed for dinner, rolled himself into the library, to which led the curtained door on the right. Sitting idly in his light, wheeled chair, ready to enter when his cousin appeared, he had heard the chat of Annon and the major. As he listened, over his usually impassive face passed varying expressions of anger, pain, bitterness, and defiance, and when the young man uttered his almost fierce "We shall see," Treherne smiled a scornful smile and clenched his pale hand with a gesture which proved that a year of suffering had not conquered the man's spirit, though it had crippled his strong body.

A singular face was Maurice Treherne's; well-cut and somewhat haughty features; a fine brow under the dark locks that carelessly streaked it; and remarkably piercing eyes. Slight in figure and wasted by pain, he still retained the grace as native to him as the stern fortitude which enabled him to hide the deep despair of an ambitious nature from every eye, and bear his affliction with a cheerful philosophy more pathetic than the most entire abandonment to grief. Carefully dressed, and with no hint at invalidism but the chair, he bore himself as easily and calmly as if the doom of lifelong helplessness did not hang over him. A single motion of the hand sent him rolling noiselessly to the curtained door, but as he did so, a voice exclaimed behind him, "Wait for me, cousin." And as he turned, a young girl approached, smiling a glad welcome as she took his hand, adding in a tone of soft reproach, "Home again, and not let me know it, till I heard the good news by accident."

"Was it good news, Octavia?" and Maurice looked up at the frank face with a new expression in those penetrating eyes of his. His cousin's open glance never changed as she stroked the hair off his forehead with the caress one often gives a child, and answered eagerly, "The best to me; the house is dull when you are away, for Jasper always becomes absorbed in horses and hounds, and leaves Mamma and me to mope by ourselves. But tell me, Maurice, what they said to you, since you would not write."

"A little hope, with time and patience. Help me to wait, dear, help me to wait."

His tone was infinitely sad, and as he spoke, he leaned his cheek against the kind hand he held, as if to find support and comfort there. The girl's face brightened beautifully, though her eyes filled, for to her alone did he betray his pain, and in her alone did he seek consolation.

"I will, I will with heart and hand! Thank heaven for the hope, and trust me it shall be fulfilled. You look very tired, Maurice. Why go in to dinner with all those people? Let me make you cozy here," she added anxiously.

"Thanks, I'd rather go in, it does me good; and if I stay away, Jasper feels that he must stay with me. I dressed in haste, am I right, little nurse?"

She gave him a comprehensive glance, daintily settled his cravat, brushed back a truant lock, and, with a maternal air that was charming, said, "My boy is always elegant, and I'm proud of him. Now we'll go in." But with her hand on the curtain she paused, saying quickly, as a voice reached her, "Who is that?"

"Frank Annon. Didn't you know he was coming?" Maurice eyed her keenly.

"No, Jasper never told me. Why did he ask him?"

"To please you."

"Me! When he knows I detest the man. No matter, I've got on the color he hates, so he won't annoy me, and Mrs. Snowdon can amuse herself with him. The general has come, you know?"

Treherne smiled, well pleased, for no sign of maiden shame or pleasure did the girl's face betray, and as he watched her while she peeped, he thought with satisfaction, Annon is right, I have the advantage, and I'll keep it at all costs.

"Here is Mamma. We must go in," said Octavia, as a stately old lady made her appearance in the drawing room.

The cousins entered together and Annon watched them covertly, while seemingly intent on paying his respects to Madame Mère, as his hostess was called by her family.

"Handsomer than ever," he muttered, as his eye rested on the blooming girl, looking more like a rose than ever in the peach-colored silk which he had once condemned because a rival admired it. She turned to reply to the major, and Annon glanced at Treherne with an irrepressible frown, for sickness had not marred the charm of that peculiar face, so colorless and thin that it seemed cut in marble; but the keen eyes shone with a wonderful brilliancy, and the whole countenance was alive with a power of intellect and will which made the observer involuntarily exclaim, "That man must suffer a daily martyrdom, so crippled and confined; if it last long he will go mad or die."

"General and Mrs. Snowden," announced the servant, and a sudden pause ensued as everyone looked up to greet the newcomers.

A feeble, white-haired old man entered, leaning on the arm of an indescribably beautiful woman. Not thirty yet, tall and nobly molded, with straight black brows over magnificent eyes; rippling dark hair gathered up in a great knot, and ornamented with a single band of gold. A sweeping dress of wine-colored velvet, set off with a dazzling neck and arms decorated like her stately head with ornaments of Roman gold. At the first glance she seemed a cold, haughty creature, born to dazzle but not to win. A deeper scrutiny detected lines of suffering in that lovely face, and behind the veil of reserve, which pride forced her to wear, appeared the anguish of a strong-willed woman burdened by a heavy cross. No one would dare express pity or offer sympathy, for her whole air repelled it, and in her gloomy eyes sat scorn of herself mingled with defiance of the scorn of others. A strange, almost tragical-looking woman, in spite of beauty, grace, and the cold sweetness of her manner. A faint smile parted her lips as she greeted those about her, and as her husband seated himself beside Lady Treherne, she lifted her head with a long breath, and a singular expression of relief, as if a burden was removed, and for the time being she was free. Sir Jasper was at her side, and as she listened, her eye glanced from face to face.

"Who is with you now?" she asked, in a low, mellow voice that was full of music.

"My sister and my cousin are yonder. You may remember Tavia as a child, she is little more now. Maurice is an invalid, but the finest fellow breathing."

"I understand," and Mrs. Snowdon's eyes softened with a sudden glance of pity for one cousin and admiration for the other, for she knew the facts.

"Major Royston, my father's friend, and Frank Annon, my own. Do you know him?" asked Sir Jasper.

"No."

"Then allow me to make him happy by presenting him, may I?"

"Not now. I'd rather see your cousin."

"Thanks, you are very kind. I'll bring him over."

"Stay, let me go to him," began the lady, with more feeling in face and voice than one would believe her capable of showing.

"Pardon, it will offend him, he will not be pitied, or relinquish any of the duties or privileges of a gentleman which he can possibly perform. He is proud, we can understand the feeling, so let us humor the poor fellow."

Mrs. Snowdon bowed silently, and Sir Jasper called out in his hearty, blunt way, as if nothing was amiss with his cousin, "Maurice, I've an honor for you. Come and receive it."

Divining what it was, Treherne noiselessly crossed the room, and with no sign of self-consciousness or embarrassment, was presented to the handsome woman. Thinking his presence might be a restraint, Sir Jasper went away. The instant his back was turned, a change came over both: an almost grim expression replaced the suavity of Treherne's face, and Mrs. Snowdon's smile faded suddenly, while a deep flush rose to her brow, as her eyes questioned his beseechingly.

"How dared you come?" he asked below his breath.

"The general insisted."

"And you could not change his purpose; poor woman!"

"You will not be pitied, neither will I," and her eyes flashed; then the fire was quenched in tears, and her voice lost all its pride in a pleading tone.

"Forgive me, I longed to see you since your illness, and so I 'dared' to come."

"You shall be gratified; look, quite helpless, crippled for life, perhaps."

The chair was turned from the groups about the fire, and as he spoke, with a bitter laugh Treherne threw back the skin which covered his knees, and showed her the useless limbs once so strong and fleet. She shrank and paled, put out her hand to arrest him, and cried in an indignant whisper, "No, no, not that! You know I never meant such cruel curiosity, such useless pain to both."

"Be still, someone is coming," he returned inaudibly; adding aloud, as he adjusted the skin and smoothed the rich fur as if speaking of it, "Yes, it is a very fine one, Jasper gave it to me. He spoils me, like a dear, generous-hearted fellow as he is. Ah, Octavia, what can I do for you?"

"Nothing, thank you. I want to recall myself to Mrs. Snowdon's memory, if she will let me."

"No need of that; I never forget happy faces and pretty pictures. Two years ago I saw you at your first ball, and longed to be a girl again."

As she spoke, Mrs. Snowdon pressed the hand shyly offered, and smiled at the spirited face before her, though the shadow in her own eyes deepened as she met the bright glance of the girl.

"How kind you were that night! I remember you let me chatter away about my family, my cousin, and my foolish little affairs with the sweetest patience, and made me very happy by your interest. I was homesick, and Aunt could never bear to hear of those things. It was before your marriage, and all the kinder, for you were the queen of the night, yet had a word for poor little me."

Mrs. Snowdon was pale to the lips, and Maurice impatiently tapped the arm of his chair, while the girl innocently chatted on.

"I am sorry the general is such an invalid; yet I dare say you find great happiness in taking care of him. It is so pleasant to be of use to those we love." And as she spoke, Octavia leaned over her cousin to hand him the glove he had dropped.

The affectionate smile that accompanied the act made the color deepen again in Mrs. Snowdon's cheek, and lit a spark in her softened eyes. Her lips curled and her voice was sweetly sarcastic as she answered, "Yes, it is charming to devote one's life to these dear invalids, and find one's reward in their gratitude. Youth, beauty, health, and happiness are small sacrifices if one wins a little comfort for the poor sufferers."

The girl felt the sarcasm under the soft words and drew back with a troubled face.

Maurice smiled, and glanced from one to the other, saying significantly, "Well for me that my little nurse loves her labor, and finds no sacrifice in it. I am fortunate in my choice."

"I trust it may prove so - " Mrs. Snowdon got no further, for at that moment dinner was announced, and Sir Jasper took her away. Annon approached with him and offered his arm to Miss Treherne, but with an air of surprise, and a little gesture of refusal, she said coldly:

"My cousin always takes me in to dinner. Be good enough to escort the major." And with her hand on the arm of the chair, she walked away with a mischievous glitter in her eyes.

Annon frowned and fell back, saying sharply, "Come, Major, what are you doing there?"

"Making discoveries."

Chapter II

Byplay

A right splendid old dowager was Lady Treherne, in her black velvet and point lace, as she sat erect and stately on a couch by the drawing-room fire, a couch which no one dare occupy in her absence, or share uninvited. The gentlemen were still over their wine, and the three ladies were alone. My lady never dozed in public, Mrs. Snowdon never gossiped, and Octavia never troubled herself to entertain any guests but those of her own age, so long pauses fell, and conversation languished, till Mrs. Snowdon roamed away into the library. As she disappeared, Lady Treherne beckoned to her daughter, who was idly making chords at the grand piano. Seating herself on the ottoman at her mother's feet, the girl took the still handsome hand in her own and amused herself with examining the old-fashioned jewels that covered it, a pretext for occupying her telltale eyes, as she suspected what was coming.

"My dear, I'm not pleased with you, and I tell you so at once, that you may amend your fault," began Madame Mère in a tender tone, for though a haughty, imperious woman, she idolized her children.

"What have I done, Mamma?" asked the girl.

"Say rather, what have you left undone. You have been very rude to Mr. Annon. It must not occur again; not only because he is a guest, but because he is your brother's friend."

My lady hesitated over the word "lover," and changed it, for to her Octavia still seemed a child, and though anxious for the alliance, she forbore to speak openly, lest the girl should turn willful, as she inherited her mother's high spirit.

"I'm sorry, Mamma. But how can I help it, when he teases me so that I detest him?" said Octavia, petulantly.

"How tease, my love?"

"Why, he follows me about like a dog, puts on a sentimental look when I appear; blushes, and beams, and bows at everything I say, if I am polite; frowns and sighs if I'm not; and glowers tragically at every man I speak to, even poor Maurice. Oh, Mamma, what foolish creatures men are!" And the girl laughed blithely, as she looked up for the first time into her mother's face.

My lady smiled, as she stroked the bright head at her knee, but asked quickly, "Why say 'even poor Maurice,' as if it were impossible for anyone to be jealous of him?"

"But isn't it, Mamma? I thought strong, well men regarded him as one set apart and done with, since his sad misfortune."

"Not entirely; while women pity and pet the poor fellow, his comrades will be jealous, absurd as it is."

"No one pets him but me, and I have a right to do it, for he is my cousin," said the girl, feeling a touch of jealousy herself.

"Rose and Blanche Talbot outdo you, my dear, and there is no cousinship to excuse them."

"Then let Frank Annon be jealous of them, and leave me in peace. They promised to come today; I'm afraid something has happened to prevent them." And Octavia gladly seized upon the new subject. But my lady was not to be eluded.

"They said they could not come till after dinner. They will soon arrive. Before they do so, I must say a few words, Tavia, and I beg you to give heed to them. I desire you to be courteous and amiable to Mr. Annon, and before strangers to be less attentive and affectionate to Maurice. You mean it kindly, but it looks ill, and causes disagreeable remarks."

"Who blames me for being devoted to my cousin? Can I ever do enough to repay him for his devotion? Mamma, you forget he saved your son's life."

Indignant tears filled the girl's eyes, and she spoke passionately, forgetting that Mrs. Snowdon was within earshot of her raised voice. With a frown my lady laid her hand on her daughter's lips, saying coldly, "I do not forget, and I religiously discharge my every obligation by every care and comfort it is in my power to bestow. You are young, romantic, and tender-hearted. You think you must give your time and health, must sacrifice your future happiness to this duty. You are wrong, and unless you learn wisdom in season, you will find that you have done harm, not good."

"God forbid! How can I do that? Tell me, and I will be wise in time."

Turning the earnest face up to her own, Lady Treherne whispered anxiously, "Has Maurice ever looked or hinted anything of love during this year he has been with us, and you his constant companion?"

"Never, Mamma; he is too honorable and too unhappy to speak or think of that. I am his little nurse, sister, and friend, no more, nor ever shall be. Do not suspect us, or put such fears into my mind, else all our comfort will be spoiled."

Flushed and eager was the girl, but her clear eyes betrayed no tender confusion as she spoke, and all her thought seemed to be to clear her cousin from the charge of loving her too well. Lady Treherne looked relieved, paused a moment, then said, seriously but gently, "This is well, but, child, I charge you tell me at once, if ever he forgets himself, for this thing cannot be. Once I hoped it might, now it is impossible; remember that he continue a friend and cousin, nothing more. I warn you in time, but if you neglect the warning, Maurice must go. No more of this; recollect my wish regarding Mr. Annon, and let your cousin amuse himself without you in public."

"Mamma, do you wish me to like Frank Annon?"

The abrupt question rather disturbed my lady, but knowing her daughter's frank, impetuous nature, she felt somewhat relieved by this candor, and answered decidedly, "I do. He is your equal in all respects; he loves you, Jasper desires it, I approve, and you, being heart-whole, can have no just objection to the alliance."

"Has he spoken to you?"

"No, to your brother."

"You wish this much, Mamma?"

"Very much, my child."

"I will try to please you, then." And stifling a sigh, the girl kissed her mother with unwonted meekness in tone and manner.

"Now I am well pleased. Be happy, my love. No one will urge or distress you. Let matters take their course, and if this hope of ours can be fulfilled, I shall be relieved of the chief care of my life."

A sound of girlish voices here broke on their ears, and springing up, Octavia hurried to meet her friends, exclaiming joyfully, "They have come! they have come!"

Two smiling, blooming girls met her at the door, and, being at an enthusiastic age, they gushed in girlish fashion for several minutes, making a pretty group as they stood in each other's arms, all talking at once, with frequent kisses and little bursts of laughter, as vents for their emotion. Madame Mère welcomed them and then went to join Mrs. Snowdon, leaving the trio to gossip unrestrained.

"My dearest creature, I thought we never should get here, for Papa had a tiresome dinner party, and we were obliged to stay, you know," cried Rose, the lively sister, shaking out the pretty dress and glancing at herself in the mirror as she fluttered about the room like a butterfly.

"We were dying to come, and so charmed when you asked us, for we haven't seen you this age, darling," added Blanche, the pensive one, smoothing her blond curls after a fresh embrace.

"I'm sorry the Ulsters couldn't come to keep Christmas with us, for we have no gentlemen but Jasper, Frank Annon, and the major. Sad, isn't it?" said Octavia, with a look of despair, which caused a fresh peal of laughter.

"One apiece, my dear, it might be worse." And Rose privately decided to appropriate Sir Jasper.

"Where is your cousin?" asked Blanche, with a sigh of sentimental interest.

"He is here, of course. I forget him, but he is not on the flirting list, you know. We must amuse him, and not expect him to amuse us, though really, all the capital suggestions and plans for merrymaking always come from him."

"He is better, I hope?" asked both sisters with real sympathy, making their young faces womanly and sweet.

"Yes, and has hopes of entire recovery. At least, they tell him so, though Dr. Ashley said there was no chance of it."

"Dear, dear, how sad! Shall we see him, Tavia?"

"Certainly; he is able to be with us now in the evening, and enjoys society as much as ever. But please take no notice of his infirmity, and make no inquiries beyond the usual 'How do you do.' He is sensitive, and hates to be considered an invalid more than ever."

"How charming it must be to take care of him, he is so accomplished and delightful. I quite envy you," said Blanche pensively.

"Sir Jasper told us that the General and Mrs. Snowdon were coming. I hope they will, for I've a most intense curiosity to see her -" began Rose.

"Hush, she is here with Mamma! Why curious? What is the mystery? For you look as if there was one," questioned Octavia under her breath.

The three charming heads bent toward one another as Rose replied in a whisper, "If I knew, I shouldn't be inquisitive. There was a rumor that she married the old general in a fit of pique, and now repents. I asked Mamma once, but she said such matters were not for young girls to hear, and not a word more would she say. N'importe, I have wits of my own, and I can satisfy myself. The gentlemen are coming! Am I all right, dear?" And the three glanced at one another with a swift scrutiny that nothing could escape, then grouped themselves prettily, and waited, with a little flutter of expectation in each young heart.

In came the gentlemen, and instantly a new atmosphere seemed to pervade the drawing room, for with the first words uttered, several romances began. Sir Jasper was taken possession of by Rose, Blanche intended to devote herself to Maurice Treherne, but Annon intercepted her, and Octavia was spared any effort at politeness by this unexpected move on the part of her lover.

"He is angry, and wishes to pique me by devoting himself to Blanche. I wish he would, with all my heart, and leave me in peace. Poor Maurice, he expects me, and I long to go to him, but must obey Mamma." And Octavia went to join the group formed by my lady, Mrs. Snowdon, the general, and the major.

The two young couples flirted in different parts of the room, and Treherne sat alone, watching them all with eyes that pierced below the surface, reading the hidden wishes, hopes, and fears that ruled them. A singular expression sat on his face as he turned from Octavia's clear countenance to Mrs. Snowdon's gloomy one. He leaned his head upon his hand and fell into deep thought, for he was passing through one of those fateful moments which come to us all, and which may make or mar a life. Such moments come when least looked for: an unexpected meeting, a peculiar mood, some trivial circumstance, or careless word produces it, and often it is gone before we realize its presence, leaving after effects to show us what we have gained or lost. Treherne was conscious that the present hour, and the acts that filled it, possessed unusual interest, and would exert an unusual influence on his life. Before him was the good and evil genius of his nature in the guise of those two women. Edith Snowdon had already tried her power, and accident only had saved him. Octavia, all unconscious as she was, never failed to rouse and stimulate the noblest attributes of mind and heart. A year spent in her society had done much for him, and he loved her with a strange mingling of passion, reverence, and gratitude. He knew why Edith Snowdon came, he felt that the old fascination had not lost its charm, and though fear was unknown to him, he was ill pleased at the sight of the beautiful, dangerous woman. On the other hand, he saw that Lady Treherne desired her daughter to shun him and smile on Annon; he acknowledged that he had no right to win the young creature, crippled and poor as he was, and a pang of jealous pain wrung his heart as he watched her.

Then a sense of power came to him, for helpless, poor, and seemingly an object of pity, he yet felt that he held the honor, peace, and happiness of nearly every person present in his hands. It was a strong temptation to this man, so full of repressed passion and power, so set apart and shut out from the more stirring duties and pleasures of life. A few words from his lips, and the pity all felt for him would be turned to fear, respect, and admiration. Why not utter them, and enjoy all that was possible? He owed the Trehernes nothing; why suffer injustice, dependence, and the compassion that wounds a proud man deepest? Wealth, love, pleasure might be his with a breath. Why not secure them now?

His pale face flushed, his eye kindled, and his thin hand lay clenched like a vise as these thoughts passed rapidly through his mind. A look, a word at that moment would sway him; he felt it, and leaned forward, waiting in secret suspense for the glance, the speech which should decide him for good or ill. Who shall say what subtle instinct caused Octavia to turn and smile at him with a wistful, friendly look that warmed his heart? He met it with an answering glance, which thrilled her strangely, for love, gratitude, and some mysterious intelligence met and mingled in the brilliant yet soft expression which swiftly shone and faded in her face. What it was she could not tell; she only felt that it filled her with an indescribable emotion never experienced before. In an instant it all passed, Lady Treherne spoke to her, and Blanche Talbot addressed Maurice, wondering, as she did so, if the enchanting smile he wore was meant for her.

"Mr. Annon having mercifully set me free, I came to try to cheer your solitude; but you look as if solitude made you happier than society does the rest of us," she said without her usual affectation, for his manner impressed her.

"You are very kind and very welcome. I do find pleasures to beguile my loneliness, which gayer people would not enjoy, and it is well that I can, else I should turn morose and tyrannical, and doom some unfortunate to entertain me all day long." He answered with a gentle courtesy which was his chief attraction to womankind.

"Pray tell me some of your devices, I'm often alone in spirit, if not so in the flesh, for Rose, though a dear girl, is not congenial, and I find no kindred soul."

A humorous glimmer came to Treherne's eyes, as the sentimental damsel beamed a soft sigh and drooped her long lashes effectively. Ignoring the topic of "kindred souls," he answered coldly, "My favorite amusement is studying the people around me. It may be rude, but tied to my corner, I cannot help watching the figures around me, and discovering their little plots and plans. I'm getting very expert, and really surprise myself sometimes by the depth of my researches."

"I can believe it; your eyes look as if they possessed that gift. Pray don't study me." And the girl shrank away with an air of genuine alarm.

Treherne smiled involuntarily, for he had read the secret of that shallow heart long ago, and was too generous to use the knowledge, however flattering it might be to him. In a reassuring tone he said, turning away the keen eyes she feared, "I give you my word I never will, charming as it might be to study the white pages of a maidenly heart. I find plenty of others to read, so rest tranquil, Miss Blanche."

"Who interests you most just now?" asked the girl, coloring with pleasure at his words. "Mrs. Snowdon looks like one who has a romance to be read, if you have the skill."

"I have read it. My lady is my study just now. I thought I knew her well, but of late she puzzles me. Human minds are more full of mysteries than any written book and more changeable than the cloud shapes in the air."

"A fine old lady, but I fear her so intensely I should never dare to try to read her, as you say." Blanche looked toward the object of discussion as she spoke, and added, "Poor Tavia, how forlorn she seems. Let me ask her to join us, may I?"

"With all my heart" was the quick reply.

Blanche glided away but did not return, for my lady kept her as well as her daughter.

"That test satisfies me; well, I submit for a time, but I think I can conquer my aunt yet." And with a patient sigh Treherne turned to observe Mrs. Snowdon.

She now stood by the fire talking with Sir Jasper, a handsome, reckless, generous-hearted young gentleman, who very plainly showed his great admiration for the lady. When he came, she suddenly woke up from her listless mood and became as brilliantly gay as she had been unmistakably melancholy before. As she chatted, she absently pushed to and fro a small antique urn of bronze on the chimneypiece, and in doing so she more than once gave Treherne a quick, significant glance, which he answered at last by a somewhat haughty nod. Then, as if satisfied, she ceased toying with the ornament and became absorbed in Sir Jasper's gallant badinage.

The instant her son approached Mrs. Snowdon, Madame Mère grew anxious, and leaving Octavia to her friends and lover, she watched Jasper. But her surveillance availed little, for she could neither see nor hear anything amiss, yet could not rid herself of the feeling that some mutual understanding existed between them. When the party broke up for the night, she lingered till all were gone but her son and nephew.

"Well, Madame Ma Mère, what troubles you?" asked Sir Jasper, as she looked anxiously into his face before bestowing her good-night kiss.

"I cannot tell, yet I feel ill at ease. Remember, my son, that you are the pride of my heart, and any sin or shame of yours would kill me. Good night, Maurice." And with a stately bow she swept away.

Lounging with both elbows on the low chimneypiece, Sir Jasper smiled at his mother's fears, and said to his cousin, the instant they were alone, "She is worried about E.S. Odd, isn't it, what instinctive antipathies women take to one another?"

"Why did you ask E.S. here?" demanded Treherne.

"My dear fellow, how could I help it? My mother wanted the general, my father's friend, and of course his wife must be asked also. I couldn't tell my mother that the lady had been a most arrant coquette, to put it mildly, and had married the old man in a pet, because my cousin and I declined to be ruined by her."

"You could have told her what mischief she makes wherever she goes, and for Octavia's sake have deferred the general's visit for a time. I warn you, Jasper, harm will come of it."

"To whom, you or me?"

"To both, perhaps, certainly to you. She was disappointed once when she lost us both by wavering between your title and my supposed fortune. She is miserable with the old man, and her only hope is in his death, for he is very feeble. You are free, and doubly attractive now, so beware, or she will entangle you before you know it."

"Thanks, Mentor. I've no fear, and shall merely amuse myself for a week, they stay no longer." And with a careless laugh, Sir Jasper strolled away.

"Much mischief may be done in a week, and this is the beginning of it," muttered Treherne, as he raised himself to look under the bronze vase for the note. It was gone!

Chapter III

Who Was It?

Who had taken it? This question tormented Treherne all that sleepless night. He suspected three persons, for only these had approached the fire after the note was hidden. He had kept his eye on it, he thought, till the stir of breaking up. In that moment it must have been removed by the major, Frank Annon, or my lady; Sir Jasper was out of the question, for he never touched an ornament in the drawing room since he had awkwardly demolished a whole étagère of costly trifles, to his mother's and sister's great grief. The major evidently suspected something, Annon was jealous, and my lady would be glad of a pretext to remove her daughter from his reach. Trusting to his skill in reading faces, he waited impatiently for morning, resolving to say nothing to anyone but Mrs. Snowdon, and from her merely to inquire what the note contained.

Treherne usually was invisible till lunch, often till dinner; therefore, fearing to excite suspicion by unwonted activity, he did not appear till noon. The mailbag had just been opened, and everyone was busy over their letters, but all looked up to exchange a word with the newcomer, and Octavia impulsively turned to meet him, then checked herself and hid her suddenly crimsoned face behind a newspaper. Treherne's eye took in everything, and saw at once in the unusually late arrival of the mail a pretext for discovering the pilferer of the note.

"All have letters but me, yet I expected one last night. Major, have you got it among yours?" And as he spoke, Treherne fixed his penetrating eyes full on the person he addressed.

With no sign of consciousness, no trace of confusion, the major carefully turned over his pile, and replied in the most natural manner, "Not a trace of it; I wish there was, for nothing annoys me more than any delay or mistake about my letters."

He knows nothing of it, thought Treherne, and turned to Annon, who was deep in a long epistle from some intimate friend, with a talent for imparting news, to judge from the reader's interest.

"Annon, I appeal to you, for I must discover who has robbed me of my letter."

"I have but one, read it, if you will, and satisfy yourself" was the brief reply.

"No, thank you. I merely asked in joke; it is doubtless among my lady's. Jasper's letters and mine often get mixed, and my lady takes care of his for him. I think you must have it, Aunt."

Lady Treherne looked up impatiently. "My dear Maurice, what a coil about a letter! We none of us have it, so do not punish us for the sins of your correspondent or the carelessness of the post."

She was not the thief, for she is always intensely polite when she intends to thwart me, thought Treherne, and, apologizing for his rudeness in disturbing them, he rolled himself to his nook in a sunny window and became apparently absorbed in a new magazine.

Mrs. Snowdon was opening the general's letters for him, and, having finished her little task, she roamed away into the library, as if in search of a book. Presently returning with one, she approached Treherne, and, putting it into his hand, said, in her musically distinct voice, "Be so kind as to find for me the passage you spoke of last night. I am curious to see it."

Instantly comprehending her stratagem, he opened it with apparent carelessness, secured the tiny note laid among the leaves, and, selecting a passage at hazard, returned her book and resumed his own. Behind the cover of it he unfolded and read these words:

I understand, but do not be anxious; the line I left was merely this, "I must see you alone, tell me when and where." No one can make much of it, and I will discover the thief before dinner. Do nothing, but watch to whom I speak first on entering, when we meet in the evening, and beware of that person.

Quietly transferring the note to the fire with the wrapper of the magazine, he dismissed the matter from his mind and left Mrs. Snowdon to play detective as she pleased, while he busied himself about his own affairs.

It was a clear, bright December day, and when the young people separated to prepare for a ride, while the general and the major sunned themselves on the terrace, Lady Treherne said to her nephew, "I am going for an airing in the pony carriage. Will you be my escort, Maurice?"

"With pleasure," replied the young man, well knowing what was in store for him.

My lady was unusually taciturn and grave, yet seemed anxious to say something which she found difficult to utter. Treherne saw this, and ended an awkward pause by dashing boldly into the subject which occupied both.

"I think you want to say something to me about Tavie, Aunt. Am I right?"

"Yes."

"Then let me spare you the pain of beginning, and prove my sincerity by openly stating the truth, as far as I am concerned. I love her very dearly, but I am not mad enough to dream of telling her so. I know that it is impossible, and I relinquish my hopes. Trust me. I will keep silent and see her marry Annon without a word of complaint, if you will it. I see by her altered manner that you have spoken to her, and that my little friend and nurse is to be mine no longer. Perhaps you are wise, but if you do this on my account, it is in vain, the mischief is done, and while I live I shall love my cousin. If you do it to spare her, I am dumb, and will go away rather than cause her a care or pain."

"Do you really mean this, Maurice?" And Lady Treherne looked at him with a changed and softened face.

Turning upon her, Treherne showed her a countenance full of suffering and sincerity, of resignation and resolve, as he said earnestly, "I do mean it; prove me in any way you please. I am not a bad fellow, Aunt, and I desire to be better. Since my misfortune I've had time to test many things, myself among others, and in spite of many faults, I do cherish the wish to keep my soul honest and true, even though my body be a wreck. It is easy to say these things, but in spite of temptation, I think I can stand firm, if you trust me."

"My dear boy, I do trust you, and thank you gratefully for this frankness. I never forget that I owe Jasper's life to you, and never expect to repay that debt. Remember this when I seem cold or unkind, and remember also that I say now, had you been spared this affliction, I would gladly have given you my girl. But -"

"But, Aunt, hear one thing," broke in Treherne. "They tell me that any sudden and violent shock of surprise, joy, or sorrow may do for me what they hope time will achieve. I said nothing of this, for it is but a chance; yet, while there is any hope, need I utterly renounce Octavia?"

"It is hard to refuse, and yet I cannot think it wise to build upon a chance so slight. Once let her have you, and both are made unhappy, if the hope fail. No, Maurice, it is better to be generous, and leave her free to make her own happiness elsewhere. Annon loves her, she is heart-whole, and will soon learn to love him, if you are silent. My poor boy, it seems cruel, but I must say it."

"Shall I go away, Aunt?" was all his answer, very firmly uttered, though his lips were white.

"Not yet, only leave them to themselves, and hide your trouble if you can. Yet, if you prefer, you shall go to town, and Benson shall see that you are comfortable. Your health will be a reason, and I will come, or write often, if you are homesick. It shall depend on you, for I want to be just and kind in this hard case. You shall decide."

"Then I will stay. I can hide my love; and to see them together will soon cease to wound me, if Octavia is happy."

"So let it rest then, for a time. You shall miss your companion as little as possible, for I will try to fill her place. Forgive me, Maurice, and pity a mother's solicitude, for these two are the last of many children, and I am a widow now."

Lady Treherne's voice faltered, and if any selfish hope or plan lingered in her nephew's mind, that appeal banished it and touched his better nature. Pressing her hand he said gently, "Dear Aunt, do not lament over me. I am one set apart for afflictions, yet I will not be conquered by them. Let us forget my youth and be friendly counselors together for the good of the two whom we both love. I must say a word about Jasper, and you will not press me to explain more than I can without breaking my promise."

"Thank you, thank you! It is regarding that woman, I know. Tell me all you can; I will not be importunate, but I disliked her the instant I saw her, beautiful and charming as she seems."

"When my cousin and I were in Paris, just before my illness, we met her. She was with her father then, a gay old man who led a life of pleasure, and was no fit guardian for a lovely daughter. She knew our story and, having fascinated both, paused to decide which she would accept: Jasper, for his title, or me, for my fortune. This was before my uncle changed his will, and I believed myself his heir; but, before she made her choice, something (don't ask me what, if you please) occurred to send us from Paris. On our return voyage we were wrecked, and then came my illness, disinheritance, and helplessness. Edith Dubarry heard the story, but rumor reported it falsely, and she believed both of us had lost the fortune. Her father died penniless, and in a moment of despair she married the general, whose wealth surrounds her with the luxury she loves, and whose failing health will soon restore her liberty -"

"And then, Maurice?" interrupted my lady.

"She hopes to win Jasper, I think."

"Never! We must prevent that at all costs. I had rather see him dead before me, than the husband of such a woman. Why is she permitted to visit homes like mine? I should have been told this sooner," exclaimed my lady angrily.

"I should have told you had I known it, and I reproved Jasper for his neglect. Do not be needlessly troubled, Aunt. There is no blemish on Mrs. Snowdon's name, and, as the wife of a brave and honorable man, she is received without question; for beauty, grace, or tact like hers can make their way anywhere. She stays but a week, and I will devote myself to her; this will save Jasper, and, if necessary, convince Tavie of my indifference -" Then he paused to stifle a sigh.

"But yourself, have you no fears for your own peace, Maurice? You must not sacrifice happiness or honor, for me or mine."

"I am safe; I love my cousin, and that is my shield. Whatever happens remember that I tried to serve you, and sincerely endeavored to forget myself."

"God bless you, my son! Let me call you so, and feel that, though I deny you my daughter, I give you heartily a mother's care and affection."

Lady Treherne was as generous as she was proud, and her nephew had conquered her by confidence and submission. He acted no part, yet, even in relinquishing all, he cherished a hope that he might yet win the heart he coveted. Silently they parted, but from that hour a new and closer bond existed between the two, and exerted an unsuspected influence over the whole household.

Maurice waited with some impatience for Mrs. Snowdon's entrance, not only because of his curiosity to see if she had discovered the thief, but because of the part he had taken upon himself to play. He was equal to it, and felt a certain pleasure in it for a threefold reason. It would serve his aunt and cousin, would divert his mind from its own cares, and, perhaps by making Octavia jealous, waken love; for, though he had chosen the right, he was but a man, and moreover a lover.

Mrs. Snowdon was late. She always was, for her toilet was elaborate, and she liked to enjoy its effects upon others. The moment she entered Treherne's eye was on her, and to his intense surprise and annoyance she addressed Octavia, saying blandly, "My dear Miss Treherne, I've been admiring your peacocks. Pray let me see you feed them tomorrow. Miss Talbot says it is a charming sight."

"If you are on the terrace just after lunch, you will find them there, and may feed them yourself, if you like" was the cool, civil reply.

"She looks like a peacock herself in that splendid green and gold dress, doesn't she?" whispered Rose to Sir Jasper, with a wicked laugh.

"Faith, so she does. I wish Tavie's birds had voices like Mrs. Snowdon's; their squalling annoys me intensely."

"I rather like it, for it is honest, and no malice or mischief is hidden behind it. I always distrust those smooth, sweet voices; they are insincere. I like a full, clear tone; sharp, if you please, but decided and true."

"Well said, Octavia. I agree with you, and your own is a perfect sample of the kind you describe." And Treherne smiled as he rolled by to join Mrs. Snowdon, who evidently waited for him, while Octavia turned to her brother to defend her pets.

"Are you sure? How did you discover?" said Maurice, affecting to admire the lady's bouquet, as he paused beside her.

"I suspected it the moment I saw her this morning. She is no actress; and dislike, distrust, and contempt were visible in her face when we met. Till you so cleverly told me my note was lost, I fancied she was disturbed about her brother, or you."

A sudden pause and a keen glance followed the last softly uttered word, but Treherne met it with an inscrutable smile and a quiet "Well, what next?"

"The moment I learned that you did not get the note I was sure she had it, and, knowing that she must have seen me put it there, in spite of her apparent innocence, I quietly asked her for it. This surprised her, this robbed the affair of any mystery, and I finished her perplexity by sending it to the major the moment she returned it to me, as if it had been intended for him. She begged pardon, said her brother was thoughtless, and she watched over him lest he should get into mischief; professed to think I meant the line for him, and behaved like a charming simpleton, as she is."

"Quite a tumult about nothing. Poor little Tavie! You doubtlessly frightened her so that we may safely correspond hereafter."

"You may give me an answer, now and here."

"Very well, meet me on the terrace tomorrow morning; the peacocks will make the meeting natural enough. I usually loiter away an hour or two there, in the sunny part of the day."

"But the girl?"

"I'll send her away."

"You speak as if it would be an easy thing to do."

"It will, both easy and pleasant."

"Now you are mysterious or uncomplimentary. You either care nothing for a tête-à-tête with her, or you will gladly send her out of my way. Which is it?"

"You shall decide. Can I have this?"

She looked at him as he touched a rose with a warning glance, for the flower was both an emblem of love and of silence. Did he mean to hint that he recalled the past, or to warn her that someone was near? She leaned from the shadow of the curtain where she sat, and caught a glimpse of a shadow gliding away.

"Who was it?" she asked, below her breath.

"A Rose," he answered, laughing. Then, as if the danger was over, he said, "How will you account to the major for the message you sent him?"

"Easily, by fabricating some interesting perplexity in which I want sage counsel. He will be flattered, and by seeming to take him into my confidence, I can hoodwink the excellent man to my heart's content, for he annoys me by his odd way of mounting guard over me at all times. Now take me in to dinner, and be your former delightful self."

"That is impossible," he said, yet proved that it was not.

Chapter IV

Feeding The Peacocks

It was indeed a charming sight, the twelve stately birds perched on the broad stone balustrade, or prancing slowly along the terrace, with the sun gleaming on their green and golden necks and the glories of their gorgeous plumes, widespread, or sweeping like rich trains behind them. In pretty contrast to the splendid creatures was their young mistress, in her simple morning dress and fur-trimmed hood and mantle, as she stood feeding the tame pets from her hand, calling their fanciful names, laughing at their pranks, and heartily enjoying the winter sunshine, the fresh wind, and the girlish pastime. As Treherne slowly approached, he watched her with lover's eyes, and found her very sweet and blithe, and dearer in his sight than ever. She had shunned him carefully all the day before, had parted at night with a hasty handshake, and had not come as usual to bid him good-morning in the library. He had taken no notice of the change as yet, but now, remembering his promise to his aunt, he resolved to let the girl know that he fully understood the relation which henceforth was to exist between them.

"Good-morning, cousin. Shall I drive you away, if I take a turn or two here?" he said, in a cheerful tone, but with a half-reproachful glance.

She looked at him an instant, then went to him with extended hand and cheeks rosier than before, while her frank eyes filled, and her voice had a traitorous tremor in it, as she said, impetuously: "I will be myself for a moment, in spite of everything. Maurice, don't think me unkind, don't reproach me, or ask my leave to come where I am. There is a reason for the change you see in me; it's not caprice, it is obedience."

"My dear girl, I know it. I meant to speak of it, and show you that I understand. Annon is a good fellow, as worthy of you as any man can be, and I wish you all the happiness you deserve."

"Do you?" And her eyes searched his face keenly.

"Yes; do you doubt it?" And so well did he conceal his love, that neither face, voice, nor manner betrayed a hint of it.

Her eyes fell, a cloud passed over her clear countenance, and she withdrew her hand, as if to caress the hungry bird that gently pecked at the basket she held. As if to change the conversation, she said playfully, "Poor Argus, you have lost your fine feathers, and so all desert you, except kind little Juno, who never forgets her friends. There, take it all, and share between you."

Treherne smiled, and said quickly, "I am a human Argus, and you have been a kind little Juno to me since I lost my plumes. Continue to be so, and you will find me a very faithful friend."

"I will." And as she answered, her old smile came back and her eyes met his again.

"Thanks! Now we shall get on happily. I don't ask or expect the old life, that is impossible. I knew that when lovers came, the friend would fall into the background; and I am content to be second, where I have so long been first. Do not think you neglect me; be happy with your lover, dear, and when you have no pleasanter amusement, come and see old Maurice."

She turned her head away, that he might not see the angry color in her cheeks, the trouble in her eyes, and when she spoke, it was to say petulantly, "I wish Jasper and Mamma would leave me in peace. I hate lovers and want none. If Frank teases, I'll go into a convent and so be rid of him."

Maurice laughed, and turned her face toward himself, saying, in his persuasive voice, "Give him a trial first, to please your mother. It can do no harm and may amuse you. Frank is already lost, and, as you are heart-whole, why not see what you can do for him? I shall have a new study, then, and not miss you so much."

"You are very kind; I'll do my best. I wish Mrs. Snowdon would come, if she is coming; I've an engagement at two, and Frank will look tragical if I'm not ready. He is teaching me billiards, and I really like the game, though I never thought I should."

"That looks well. I hope you'll learn a double lesson, and Annon find a docile pupil in both."

"You are very pale this morning; are you in pain, Maurice?" suddenly asked Octavia, dropping the tone of assumed ease and gaiety under which she had tried to hide her trouble.

"Yes, but it will soon pass. Mrs. Snowdon is coming. I saw her at the hall door a moment ago. I will show her the peacocks, if you want to go. She won't mind the change, I dare say, as you don't like her, and I do."

"No, I am sure of that. It was an arrangement, perhaps? I understand. I will not play Mademoiselle De Trop."

Sudden fire shone in the girl's eyes, sudden contempt curled her lip, and a glance full of meaning went from her cousin to the door, where Mrs. Snowdon appeared, waiting for her maid to bring her some additional wrappings.

"You allude to the note you stole. How came you to play that prank, Tavie?" asked Treherne tranquilly.

"I saw her put it under the urn. I thought it was for Jasper, and I took it," she said boldly.

"Why for Jasper?"

"I remembered his speaking of meeting her long ago, and describing her beauty enthusiastically, and so did you."

"You have a good memory."

"I have for everything concerning those I love. I observed her manner of meeting my brother, his devotion to her, and, when they stood laughing together before the fire, I felt sure that she wished to charm him again."

"Again? Then she did charm him once?" asked Treherne, anxious to know how much Jasper had told his sister.

"He always denied it, and declared that you were the favorite."

"Then why not think the note for me?" he asked.

"I do now" was the sharp answer.

"But she told you it was for the major, and sent it."

"She deceived me; I am not surprised. I am glad Jasper is safe, and I wish you a pleasant tête-à-tête."

Bowing with unwonted dignity, Octavia set down her basket, and walked away in one direction as Mrs. Snowdon approached in another.

"I have done it now," sighed Treherne, turning from the girlish figure to watch the stately creature who came sweeping toward him with noiseless grace.

Brilliancy and splendor became Mrs. Snowdon; she enjoyed luxury, and her beauty made many things becoming which in a plainer woman would have been out of taste, and absurd. She had wrapped herself in a genuine Eastern burnous of scarlet, blue, and gold; the hood drawn over her head framed her fine face in rich hues, and the great gilt tassels shone against her rippling black hair. She wore it with grace, and the barbaric splendor of the garment became her well. The fresh air touched her cheeks with a delicate color; her usually gloomy eyes were brilliant now, and the smile that parted her lips was full of happiness.

"Welcome, Cleopatra!" cried Treherne, with difficulty repressing a laugh, as the peacocks screamed and fled before the rustling amplitude of her drapery.

"I might reply by calling you Thaddeus of Warsaw, for you look very romantic and Polish with your pale, pensive face, and your splendid furs," she answered, as she paused beside him with admiration very visibly expressed in her eyes.

Treherne disliked the look, and rather abruptly said, as he offered her the basket of bread, "I have disposed of my cousin, and offered to do the honors of the peacocks. Here they are, will you feed them?"

"No, thank you, I care nothing for the fowls, as you know; I came to speak to you," she said impatiently.

"I am at your service."

"I wish to ask you a question or two, is it permitted?"

"What man ever refused Mrs. Snowdon a request?"

"Nay, no compliments; from you they are only satirical evasions. I was deceived when abroad, and rashly married that old man. Tell me truly how things stand."

"Jasper has all. I have nothing."

"I am glad of it."

"Many thanks for the hearty speech. You at least speak sincerely," he said bitterly.

"I do, Maurice, I do; let me prove it."

Treherne's chair was close beside the balustrade. Mrs. Snowdon leaned on the carved railing, with her back to the house and her face screened by a tall urn. Looking steadily at him, she said rapidly and low, "You thought I wavered between you and Jasper, when we parted two years ago. I did; but it was not between title and fortune that I hesitated. It was between duty and love. My father, a fond, foolish old man, had set his heart on seeing me a lady. I was his all; my beauty was his delight, and no untitled man was deemed worthy of me. I loved him tenderly. You may doubt this, knowing how selfish, reckless, and vain I am, but I have a heart, and with better training had been a better woman. No matter, it is too late now. Next my father, I loved you. Nay, hear me, I will clear myself in your eyes. I mean no wrong to the general. He is kind, indulgent, generous; I respect him, I am grateful, and while he lives, I shall be true to him."

"Then be silent now. Do not recall the past, Edith; let it sleep, for both our sakes," began Treherne; but she checked him imperiously.

"It shall, when I am done. I loved you, Maurice; for, of all the gay, idle, pleasure-seeking men I saw about me, you were the only one who seemed to have a thought beyond the folly of the hour. Under the seeming frivolity of your life lay something noble, heroic, and true. I felt that you had a purpose, that your present mood was but transitory, a young man's holiday, before the real work of his life began. This attracted, this won me; for even in the brief regard you then gave me, there was an earnestness no other man had shown. I wanted your respect; I longed to earn your love, to share your life, and prove that even in my neglected nature slept the power of canceling a frivolous past by a noble future. Oh, Maurice, had you lingered one week more, I never should have been the miserable thing I am!"

There her voice faltered and failed, for all the bitterness of lost love, peace, and happiness sounded in the pathetic passion of that exclamation. She did not weep, for tears seldom dimmed those tragical eyes of hers; but she wrung her hands in mute despair, and looked down into the frost-blighted gardens below, as if she saw there a true symbol of her own ruined life. Treherne uttered not a word, but set his teeth with an almost fierce glance toward the distant figure of Sir Jasper, who was riding gaily away, like one unburdened by a memory or a care.

Hurriedly Mrs. Snowdon went on, "My father begged and commanded me to choose your cousin. I could not break his heart, and asked for time, hoping to soften him. While I waited, that mysterious affair hurried you from Paris, and then came the wreck, the illness, and the rumor that old Sir Jasper had disinherited both nephews. They told me you were dying, and I became a passive instrument in my father's hands. I promised to recall and accept your cousin, but the old man died before it was done, and then I cared not what became of me.

"General Snowdon was my father's friend; he pitied me; he saw my desolate, destitute state, my despair and helplessness. He comforted, sustained, and saved me. I was grateful; and when he offered me his heart and home, I accepted them. He knew I had no love to give; but as a friend, a daughter, I would gladly serve him, and make his declining years as happy as I could. It was all over, when I heard that you were alive, afflicted, and poor. I longed to come and live for you. My new bonds became heavy fetters then, my wealth oppressed me, and I was doubly wretched, for I dared not tell my trouble, and it nearly drove me mad. I have seen you now; I know that you are happy; I read your cousin's love and see a peaceful life in store for you. This must content me, and I must learn to bear it as I can."

She paused, breathless and pale, and walked rapidly along the terrace, as if to hide or control the agitation that possessed her.

Treherne still sat silent, but his heart leaped within him, as he thought, "She sees that Octavia loves me! A woman's eye is quick to detect love in another, and she asserts what I begin to hope. My cousin's manner just now, her dislike of Annon, her new shyness with me; it may be true, and if it is, Heaven help me, what am I saying! I must not hope, nor wish, nor dream; I must renounce and forget."

He leaned his head upon his hand, and sat so still Mrs. Snowdon rejoined him, pale, but calm and self-possessed. As she drew near, she marked his attitude, the bitter sadness of his face, and hope sprang up within her. Perhaps she was mistaken; perhaps he did not love his cousin; perhaps he still remembered the past, and still regretted the loss of the heart she had just laid bare before him. Her husband was failing, and might die any day. And then, free, rich, beautiful, and young, what might she not become to Treherne, helpless, poor, and ambitious? With all her faults, she was generous, and this picture charmed her fancy, warmed her heart, and comforted her pain.

"Maurice," she said softly, pausing again beside him, "if I mistake you and your hopes, it is because I dare ask nothing for myself; but if ever a time shall come when I have liberty to give or help, ask of me anything, and it is gladly yours."

He understood her, pitied her, and, seeing that she found consolation in a distant hope, he let her enjoy it while she might. Gravely, yet gratefully, he spoke, and pressed the hand extended to him with an impulsive gesture.

"Generous as ever, Edith, and impetuously frank. Thank you for your sincerity, your kindness, and the affection you once gave me. I say 'once,' for now duty, truth, and honor bar us from each other. My life must be solitary, yet I shall find work to do, and learn to be content. You owe all devotion to the good old man who loves you, and will not fail him, I am sure. Leave the future and the past, but let us make the present what it may be, a time to forgive and forget, to take heart and begin anew. Christmas is a fitting time for such resolves, and the birth of friendship such as ours may be."

Something in his tone and manner struck her, and, eyeing him with soft wonder, she exclaimed, "How changed you are!"

"Need you tell me that?" And he glanced at his helpless limbs with a bitter yet pathetic look of patience.

"No, no, not so! I mean in mind, not body. Once you were gay and careless, eager and fiery, like Jasper; now you are grave and quiet, or cheerful, and so very kind. Yet, in spite of illness and loss, you seem twice the man you were, and something wins respect, as well as admiration, and love."

Her dark eyes filled as the last word left her lips, and the beauty of a touched heart shone in her face. Maurice looked up quickly, asking with sudden earnestness, "Do you see it? Then it is true. Yes, I am changed, thank God! And she has done it."

"Who?" demanded his companion jealously.

"Octavia. Unconsciously, yet surely, she has done much for me, and this year of seeming loss and misery has been the happiest, most profitable of my life. I have often heard that afflictions were the best teachers, and I believe it now."

Mrs. Snowdon shook her head sadly.

"Not always; they are tormentors to some. But don't preach, Maurice. I am still a sinner, though you incline to sainthood, and I have one question more to ask. What was it that took you and Jasper so suddenly away from Paris?"

"That I can never tell you."

"I shall discover it for myself, then."

"It is impossible."

"Nothing is impossible to a determined woman."

"You can neither wring, surprise, nor bribe this secret from the two persons who hold it. I beg of you to let it rest," said Treherne earnestly.

"I have a clue, and I shall follow it; for I am convinced that something is wrong, and you are -"

"Dear Mrs. Snowdon, are you so charmed with the birds that you forget your fellow-beings, or so charmed with one fellow-being that you forget the birds?"

As the sudden question startled both, Rose Talbot came along the terrace, with hands full of holly and a face full of merry mischief, adding as she vanished, "I shall tell Tavie that feeding the peacocks is such congenial amusement for lovers, she and Mr. Annon had better try it."

"Saucy gypsy!" muttered Treherne.

But Mrs. Snowdon said, with a smile of double meaning, "Many a true word is spoken in jest."

Chapter V

Under The Mistletoe

Unusually gay and charming the three young friends looked, dressed alike in fleecy white with holly wreaths in their hair, as they slowly descended the wide oaken stairway arm in arm. A footman was lighting the hall lamps, for the winter dusk gathered early, and the girls were merrily chatting about the evening's festivity when suddenly a loud, long shriek echoed through the hall. A heavy glass shade fell from the man's hand with a crash, and the young ladies clung to one another aghast, for mortal terror was in the cry, and a dead silence followed it.

"What was it, John?" demanded Octavia, very pale, but steady in a moment.

"I'll go and see, miss." And the man hurried away.

"Where did the dreadful scream come from?" asked Rose, collecting her wits as rapidly as possible.

"Above us somewhere. Oh, let us go down among people; I am frightened to death," whispered Blanche, trembling and faint.

Hurrying into the parlor, they found only Annon and the major, both looking startled, and both staring out of the windows.

"Did you hear it? What could it be? Don't go and leave us!" cried the girls in a breath, as they rushed in.

The gentlemen had heard, couldn't explain the cry, and were quite ready to protect the pretty creatures who clustered about them like frightened fawns. John speedily appeared, looking rather wild, and as eager to tell his tale as they to listen.

"It's Patty, one of the maids, miss, in a fit. She went up to the north gallery to see that the fires was right, for it takes a power of wood to warm the gallery even enough for dancing, as you know, miss. Well, it was dark, for the fires was low and her candle went out as she whisked open the door, being flurried, as the maids always is when they go in there. Halfway down the gallery she says she heard a rustling, and stopped. She's the pluckiest of 'em all, and she called out, 'I see you!' thinking it was some of us trying to fright her. Nothing answered, and she went on a bit, when suddenly the fire flared up one flash, and there right before her was the ghost."

"Don't be foolish, John. Tell us what it was," said Octavia sharply, though her face whitened and her heart sank as the last word passed the man's lips.

"It was a tall, black figger, miss, with a dead-white face and a black hood. She see it plain, and turned to go away, but she hadn't gone a dozen steps when there it was again before her, the same tall, dark thing with the dead-white face looking out from the black hood. It lifted its arm as if to hold her, but she gave a spring and dreadful screech, and ran to Mrs. Benson's room, where she dropped in a fit."

"How absurd to be frightened by the shadows of the figures in armor that stand along the gallery!" said Rose, boldly enough, though she would have declined entering the gallery without a light.

"Nay, I don't wonder, it's a ghostly place at night. How is the poor thing?" asked Blanche, still hanging on the major's arm in her best attitude.

"If Mamma knows nothing of it, tell Mrs. Benson to keep it from her, please. She is not well, and such things annoy her very much," said Octavia, adding as the man turned away, "Did anyone look in the gallery after Patty told her tale?"

"No, miss. I'll go and do it myself; I'm not afraid of man, ghost, or devil, saving your presence, ladies," replied John.

"Where is Sir Jasper?" suddenly asked the major.

"Here I am. What a deuce of a noise someone has been making. It disturbed a capital dream. Why, Tavie, what is it?" And Sir Jasper came out of the library with a sleepy face and tumbled hair.

They told him the story, whereat he laughed heartily, and said the maids were a foolish set to be scared by a shadow. While he still laughed and joked, Mrs. Snowdon entered, looking alarmed, and anxious to know the cause of the confusion.

"How interesting! I never knew you kept a ghost. Tell me all about it, Sir Jasper, and soothe our nerves by satisfying our curiosity," she said in her half-persuasive, half-commanding way, as she seated herself on Lady Treherne's sacred sofa.

"There's not much to tell, except that this place used to be an abbey, in fact as well as in name. An ancestor founded it, and for years the monks led a jolly life here, as one may see, for the cellar is twice as large as the chapel, and much better preserved. But another ancestor, a gay and gallant baron, took a fancy to the site for his castle, and, in spite of prayers, anathemas, and excommunication, he turned the poor fellows out, pulled down the abbey, and built this fine old place. Abbot Boniface, as he left his abbey, uttered a heavy curse on all who should live here, and vowed to haunt us till the last Treherne vanished from the face of the earth. With this amiable threat the old party left Baron Roland to his doom, and died as soon as he could in order to begin his cheerful mission."

"Did he haunt the place?" asked Blanche eagerly.

"Yes, most faithfully from that time to this. Some say many of the monks still glide about the older parts of the abbey, for Roland spared the chapel and the north gallery which joined it to the modern building. Poor fellows, they are welcome, and once a year they shall have a chance to warm their ghostly selves by the great fires always kindled at Christmas in the gallery."

"Mrs. Benson once told me that when the ghost walked, it was a sure sign of a coming death in the family. Is that true?" asked Rose, whose curiosity was excited by the expression of Octavia's face, and a certain uneasiness in Sir Jasper's manner in spite of his merry mood.

"There is a stupid superstition of that sort in the family, but no one except the servants believes it, of course. In times of illness some silly maid or croaking old woman can easily fancy they see a phantom, and, if death comes, they are sure of the ghostly warning. Benson saw it before my father died, and old Roger, the night my uncle was seized with apoplexy. Patty will never be made to believe that this warning does not forebode the death of Maurice or myself, for the gallant spirit leaves the ladies of our house to depart in peace. How does it strike you, Cousin?"

Turning as he spoke, Sir Jasper glanced at Treherne, who had entered while he spoke.

"I am quite skeptical and indifferent to the whole affair, but I agree with Octavia that it is best to say nothing to my aunt if she is ignorant of the matter. Her rooms are a long way off, and perhaps she did not hear the confusion."

"You seem to hear everything; you were not with us when I said that." And Octavia looked up with an air of surprise.

Smiling significantly, Treherne answered, "I hear, see, and understand many things that escape others. Jasper, allow me to advise you to smooth the hair which your sleep has disarranged. Mrs. Snowdon, permit me. This rich velvet catches the least speck." And with his handkerchief he delicately brushed away several streaks of white dust which clung to the lady's skirt.

Sir Jasper turned hastily on his heel and went to remake his toilet; Mrs. Snowdon bit her lip, but thanked Treherne sweetly and begged him to fasten her glove. As he did so, she said softly, "Be more careful next time. Octavia has keen eyes, and the major may prove inconvenient."

"I have no fear that you will," he whispered back, with a malicious glance.

Here the entrance of my lady put an end to the ghostly episode, for it was evident that she knew nothing of it. Octavia slipped away to question John, and learn that no sign of a phantom was to be seen. Treherne devoted himself to Mrs. Snowdon, and the major entertained my lady, while Sir Jasper and the girls chatted apart.

It was Christmas Eve, and a dance in the great gallery was the yearly festival at the abbey. All had been eager for it, but the maid's story seemed to have lessened their enthusiasm, though no one would own it. This annoyed Sir Jasper, and he exerted himself to clear the atmosphere by affecting gaiety he did not feel. The moment the gentlemen came in after dinner he whispered to his mother, who rose, asked the general for his arm, and led the way to the north gallery, whence the sound of music now proceeded. The rest followed in a merry procession, even Treherne, for two footmen carried him up the great stairway, chair and all.

Nothing could look less ghostly now than the haunted gallery. Fires roared up a wide chimney at either end, long rows of figures clad in armor stood on each side, one mailed hand grasping a lance, the other bearing a lighted candle, a device of Sir Jasper's. Narrow windows pierced in the thick walls let in gleams of wintry moonlight; ivy, holly, and evergreen glistened in the ruddy glow of mingled firelight and candle shine. From the arched stone roof hung tattered banners, and in the midst depended a great bunch of mistletoe. Red-cushioned seats stood in recessed window nooks, and from behind a high-covered screen of oak sounded the blithe air of Sir Roger de Coverley.

With the utmost gravity and stateliness my lady and the general led off the dance, for, according to the good old fashion, the men and maids in their best array joined the gentlefolk and danced with their betters in a high state of pride and bashfulness. Sir Jasper twirled the old housekeeper till her head spun around and around and her decorous skirts rustled stormily; Mrs. Snowdon captivated the gray-haired butler by her condescension; and John was made a proud man by the hand of his young mistress. The major came out strong among the pretty maids, and Rose danced the footmen out of breath long before the music paused.

The merriment increased from that moment, and when the general surprised my lady by gallantly saluting her as she unconsciously stood under the mistletoe, the applause was immense. Everyone followed the old gentleman's example as fast as opportunities occurred, and the young ladies soon had as fine a color as the housemaids. More dancing, games, songs, and all manner of festival devices filled the evening, yet under cover of the gaiety more than one little scene was enacted that night, and in an hour of seeming frivolity the current of several lives was changed.

By a skillful maneuver Annon led Octavia to an isolated recess, as if to rest after a brisk game, and, taking advantage of the auspicious hour, pleaded his suit. She heard him patiently and, when he paused, said slowly, yet decidedly, and with no sign of maiden hesitation, "Thanks for the honor you do me, but I cannot accept it, for I do not love you. I think I never can."

"Have you tried?" he asked eagerly.

"Yes, indeed I have. I like you as a friend, but no more. I know Mamma desires it, that Jasper hopes for it, and I try to please them, but love will not be forced, so what can I do?" And she smiled in spite of herself at her own blunt simplicity.

"No, but it can be cherished, strengthened, and in time won, with patience and devotion. Let me try, Octavia; it is but fair, unless you have already learned from another the lesson I hope to teach. Is it so?"

"No, I think not. I do not understand myself as yet, I am so young, and this so sudden. Give me time, Frank."

She blushed and fluttered now, looked half angry, half beseeching, and altogether lovely.

"How much time shall I give? It cannot take long to read a heart like yours, dear." And fancying her emotion a propitious omen, he assumed the lover in good earnest.

"Give me time till the New Year. I will answer then, and, meantime, leave me free to study both myself and you. We have known each other long, I own, but, still, this changes everything, and makes you seem another person. Be patient, Frank, and I will try to make my duty a pleasure."

"I will. God bless you for the kind hope, Octavia. It has been mine for years, and if I lose it, it will go hardly with me."

Later in the evening General Snowdon stood examining the antique screen. In many places carved oak was pierced quite through, so that voices were audible from behind it. The musicians had gone down to supper, the young folk were quietly busy at the other end of the hall, and as the old gentleman admired the quaint carving, the sound of his own name caught his ear. The housekeeper and butler still remained, though the other servants had gone, and sitting cosily behind the screen chatted in low tones believing themselves secure.

"It was Mrs. Snowdon, Adam, as I'm a living woman, though I wouldn't say it to anyone but you. She and Sir Jasper were here wrapped in cloaks, and up to mischief, I'll be bound. She is a beauty, but I don't envy her, and there'll be trouble in the house if she stays long."

"But how do you know, Mrs. Benson, she was here? Where's your proof, mum?" asked the pompous butler.

"Look at this, and then look at the outlandish trimming of the lady's dress. You men are so dull about such matters you'd never observe these little points. Well, I was here first after Patty, and my light shone on this jet ornament lying near where she saw the spirit. No one has any such tasty trifles but Mrs. Snowdon, and these are all over her gown. If that ain't proof, what is?"

"Well, admitting it, I then say what on earth should she and Master be up here for, at such a time?" asked the slow-witted butler.

"Adam, we are old servants of the family, and to you I'll say what tortures shouldn't draw from to another. Master has been wild, as you know, and it's my belief that he loved this lady abroad. There was a talk of some mystery, or misdeed, or misfortune, more than a year ago, and she was in it. I'm loath to say it, but I think Master loves her still, and she him. The general is an old man, she is but young, and so spirited and winsome she can't in reason care for him as for a fine, gallant gentleman like Sir Jasper. There's trouble brewing, Adam, mark my words. There's trouble brewing for the Trehernes."

So low had the voices fallen that the listener could not have caught the words had not his ear been strained to the utmost. He did hear all, and his wasted face flashed with the wrath of a young man, then grew pale and stern as he turned to watch his wife. She stood apart from the others talking to Sir Jasper, who looked unusually handsome and debonair as he fanned her with a devoted air.

Perhaps it is true, thought the old man bitterly. They are well matched, were lovers once, no doubt, and long to be so again. Poor Edith, I was very blind. And with his gray head bowed upon his breast the general stole away, carrying an arrow in his brave old heart.

"Blanche, come here and rest, you will be ill tomorrow; and I promised Mamma to take care of you."

With which elder-sisterly command Rose led the girl to an immense old chair, which held them both.

"Now listen to me and follow my advice, for I am wise in my generation, though not yet gray. They are all busy, so leave them alone and let me show you what is to be done."

Rose spoke softly, but with great resolution, and nodded her pretty head so energetically that the holly berries came rolling over her white shoulders.

"We are not as rich as we might be, and must establish ourselves as soon and as well as possible. I intend to be Lady Treherne. You can be the Honorable Mrs. Annon, if you give your mind to it."

"My dear child, are you mad?" whispered Blanche.

"Far from it, but you will be if you waste your time on Maurice. He is poor, and a cripple, though very charming, I admit. He loves Tavie, and she will marry him, I am sure. She can't endure Frank, but tries to because my lady commands it. Nothing will come of it, so try your fascinations and comfort the poor man; sympathy now will foster love hereafter."

"Don't talk so here, Rose, someone will hear us," began her sister, but the other broke in briskly.

"No fear, a crowd is the best place for secrets. Now remember what I say, and make your game while the ball is rolling. Other people are careful not to put their plans into words, but I'm no hypocrite, and say plainly what I mean. Bear my sage counsel in mind and act wisely. Now come and begin."

Treherne was sitting alone by one of the great fires, regarding the gay scene with serious air. For him there was neither dancing nor games; he could only roam about catching glimpses of forbidden pleasures, impossible delights, and youthful hopes forever lost to him. Sad but not morose was his face, and to Octavia it was a mute reproach which she could not long resist. Coming up as if to warm herself, she spoke to him in her usually frank and friendly way, and felt her heart beat fast when she saw how swift a change her cordial manner wrought in him.

"How pretty your holly is! Do you remember how we used to go and gather it for festivals like this, when we were happy children?" he asked, looking up at her with eyes full of tender admiration.

"Yes, I remember. Everyone wears it tonight as a badge, but you have none. Let me get you a bit, I like to have you one of us in all things."

She leaned forward to break a green sprig from the branch over the chimneypiece; the strong draft drew in her fleecy skirt, and in an instant she was enveloped in flames.

"Maurice, save me, help me!" cried a voice of fear and agony, and before anyone could reach her, before he himself knew how the deed was done, Treherne had thrown himself from his chair, wrapped the tiger skin tightly about her, and knelt there clasping her in his arms heedless of fire, pain, or the incoherent expressions of love that broke from his lips.

Chapter VI

Miracles

Great was the confusion and alarm which reigned for many minutes, but when the panic subsided two miracles appeared. Octavia was entirely uninjured, and Treherne was standing on his feet, a thing which for months he had not done without crutches. In the excitement of the moment, no one observed the wonder; all were crowding about the girl, who, pale and breathless but now self-possessed, was the first to exclaim, pointing to her cousin, who had drawn himself up, with the help of his chair, and leaned there smiling, with a face full of intense delight.

"Look at Maurice! Oh, Jasper, help him or he'll fall!"

Sir Jasper sprung to his side and put a strong arm about him, while a chorus of wonder, sympathy, and congratulations rose about them.

"Why, lad, what does it mean? Have you been deceiving us all this time?" cried Jasper, as Treherne leaned on him, looking exhausted but truly happy.

"It means that I am not to be a cripple all my life; that they did not deceive me when they said a sudden shock might electrify me with a more potent magnetism than any they could apply. It has, and if I am cured I owe it all to you, Octavia."

He stretched his hands to her with a gesture of such passionate gratitude that the girl covered her face to hide its traitorous tenderness, and my lady went to him, saying brokenly, as she embraced him with maternal warmth, "God bless you for this act, Maurice, and reward you with a perfect cure. To you I owe the lives of both my children; how can I thank you as I ought?"

"I dare not tell you yet," he whispered eagerly, then added, "I am growing faint, Aunt. Get me away before I make a scene."

This hint recalled my lady to her usual state of dignified self-possession. Bidding Jasper and the major help Treherne to his room without delay, she begged Rose to comfort her sister, who was sobbing hysterically, and as they all obeyed her, she led her daughter away to her own apartment, for the festivities of the evening were at an end.

At the same time Mrs. Snowdon and Annon bade my lady good-night, as if they also were about to retire, but as they reached the door of the gallery Mrs. Snowdon paused and beckoned Annon back. They were alone now, and, standing before the fire which had so nearly made that Christmas Eve a tragical one, she turned to him with a face full of interest and sympathy as she said, nodding toward the blackened shreds of Octavia's dress, and the scorched tiger skin which still lay at their feet, "That was both a fortunate and an unfortunate little affair, but I fear Maurice's gain will be your loss. Pardon my frankness for Octavia's sake; she is a fine creature, and I long to see her given to one worthy of her. I am a woman to read faces quickly; I know that your suit does not prosper as you would have it, and I desire to help you. May I?"

"Indeed you may, and command any service of me in return. But to what do I owe this unexpected friendliness?" cried Annon, both grateful and surprised.

"To my regard for the young lady, my wish to save her from an unworthy man."

"Do you mean Treherne?" asked Annon, more and more amazed.

"I do. Octavia must not marry a gambler!"

"My dear lady, you labor under some mistake; Treherne is by no means a gambler. I owe him no goodwill, but I cannot hear him slandered."

"You are generous, but I am not mistaken. Can you, on your honor, assure me that Maurice never played?"

Mrs. Snowdon's keen eyes were on him, and he looked embarrassed for a moment, but answered with some hesitation, "Why, no, I cannot say that, but I can assure you that he is not an habitual gambler. All young men of his rank play more or less, especially abroad. It is merely an amusement with most, and among men is not considered dishonorable or dangerous. Ladies think differently, I believe, at least in England."

At the word "abroad," Mrs. Snowdon's face brightened, and she suddenly dropped her eyes, as if afraid of betraying some secret purpose.

"Indeed we do, and well we may, many of us having suffered from this pernicious habit. I have had special cause to dread and condemn it, and the fear that Octavia should in time suffer what I have suffered as a girl urges me to interfere where otherwise I should be dumb. Mr. Annon, there was a rumor that Maurice was forced to quit Paris, owing to some dishonorable practices at the gaming table. Is this true?"

"Nay, don't ask me; upon my soul I cannot tell you. I only know that something was amiss, but what I never learned. Various tales were whispered at the clubs, and Sir Jasper indignantly denied them all. The bravery with which Maurice saved his cousin, and the sad affliction which fell upon him, silenced the gossip, and it was soon forgotten."

Mrs. Snowdon remained silent for a moment, with brows knit in deep thought, while Annon uneasily watched her. Suddenly she glanced over her shoulder, drew nearer, and whispered cautiously, "Did the rumors of which you speak charge him with -" and the last word was breathed into Annon's ear almost inaudibily.

He started, as if some new light broke on him, and stared at the speaker with a troubled face for an instant, saying hastily, "No, but now you remind me that when an affair of that sort was discussed the other day Treherne looked very odd, and rolled himself away, as if it didn't interest him. I can't believe it, and yet it may be something of the kind. That would account for old Sir Jasper's whim, and Treherne's steady denial of any knowledge of the cause. How in heaven's name did you learn this?"

"My woman's wit suggested it, and my woman's will shall confirm or destroy the suspicion. My lady and Octavia evidently know nothing, but they shall if there is any danger of the girl's being won by him."

"You would not tell her!" exclaimed Annon.

"I will, unless you do it" was the firm answer.

"Never! To betray a friend, even to gain the woman I love, is a thing I cannot do; my honor forbids it."

Mrs. Snowdon smiled scornfully.

"Men's code of honor is a strong one, and we poor women suffer from it. Leave this to me; do your best, and if all other means fail, you may be glad to try my device to prevent Maurice from marrying his cousin. Gratitude and pity are strong allies, and if he recovers, his strong will will move heaven and earth to gain her. Good night." And leaving her last words to rankle in Annon's mind, Mrs. Snowdon departed to endure sleepless hours full of tormenting memories, newborn hopes, and alternations of determination and despair.

Treherne's prospect of recovery filled the whole house with delight, for his patient courage and unfailing cheerfulness had endeared him to all. It was no transient amendment, for day by day he steadily gained strength and power, passing rapidly from chair to crutches, from crutches to a cane and a friend's arm, which was always ready for him. Pain returned with returning vitality, but he bore it with a fortitude that touched all who witnessed it. At times motion was torture, yet motion was necessary lest the torpidity should return, and Treherne took his daily exercise with unfailing perseverance, saying with a smile, though great drops stood upon his forehead, "I have something dearer even than health to win. Hold me up, Jasper, and let me stagger on, in spite of everything, till my twelve turns are made."

He remembered Lady Treherne's words, "If you were well, I'd gladly give my girl to you." This inspired him with strength, endurance, and a happiness which could not be concealed. It overflowed in looks, words, and acts; it infected everyone, and made these holidays the blithest the old abbey had seen for many a day.

Annon devoted himself to Octavia, and in spite of her command to be left in peace till the New Year, she was very kind, so kind that hope flamed up in his heart, though he saw that something like compassion often shone on him from her frank eyes, and her compliance had no touch of the tender docility which lovers long to see. She still avoided Treherne, but so skillfully that few observed the change but Annon and himself. In public Sir Jasper appeared to worship at the sprightly Rose's shrine, and she fancied her game was prospering well.

But had any one peeped behind the scenes it would have been discovered that during the half hour before dinner, when everyone was in their dressing rooms and the general taking his nap, a pair of ghostly black figures flitted about the haunted gallery, where no servant ventured without orders. The major fancied himself the only one who had made this discovery, for Mrs. Snowdon affected Treherne's society in public, and was assiduous in serving and amusing the "dear convalescent," as she called him. But the general did not sleep; he too watched and waited, longing yet dreading to speak, and hoping that this was but a harmless freak of Edith's, for her caprices were many, and till now he had indulged them freely. This hesitation disgusted the major, who, being a bachelor, knew little of women's ways, and less of their powers of persuasion. The day before New Year he took a sudden resolution, and demanded a private interview with the general.

"I have come on an unpleasant errand, sir," he abruptly began, as the old man received him with an expression which rather daunted the major. "My friendship for Lady Treherne, and my guardianship of her children, makes me jealous of the honor of the family. I fear it is in danger, sir; pardon me for saying it, but your wife is the cause."

"May I trouble you to explain, Major Royston" was all the general's reply, as his old face grew stern and haughty.

"I will, sir, briefly. I happen to know from Jasper that there were love passages between Miss Dubarry and himself a year or more ago in Paris. A whim parted them, and she married. So far no reproach rests upon either, but since she came here it has been evident to others as well as myself that Jasper's affection has revived, and that Mrs. Snowdon does not reject and reprove it as she should. They often meet, and from Jasper's manner I am convinced that mischief is afloat. He is ardent, headstrong, and utterly regardless of the world's opinion in some cases. I have watched them, and what I tell you is true."

"Prove it."

"I will. They meet in the north gallery, wrapped in dark cloaks, and play ghost if anyone comes. I concealed myself behind the screen last evening at dusk, and satisfied myself that my suspicions were correct. I heard little of their conversation, but that little was enough."

"Repeat it, if you please."

"Sir Jasper seemed pleading for some promise which she reluctantly gave, saying, 'While you live I will be true to my word with everyone but him. He will suspect, and it will be useless to keep it from him.'

"'He will shoot me for this if he knows I am the traitor,' expostulated Jasper.

"'He shall not know that; I can hoodwink him easily, and serve my purpose also.'

"'You are mysterious, but I leave all to you and wait for my reward. When shall I have it, Edith?' She laughed, and answered so low I could not hear, for they left the gallery as they spoke. Forgive me, General, for the pain I inflict. You are the only person to whom I have spoken, and you are the only person who can properly and promptly prevent this affair from bringing open shame and scandal on an honorable house. To you I leave it, and will do my part with this infatuated young man if you will withdraw the temptation which will ruin him."

"I will. Thank you, Major. Trust to me, and by tomorrow I will prove that I can act as becomes me."

The grief and misery in the general's face touched the major; he silently wrung his hand and went away, thanking heaven more fervently than ever that no cursed coquette of a woman had it in her power to break his heart.

While this scene was going on above, another was taking place in the library. Treherne sat there alone, thinking happy thoughts evidently, for his eyes shone and his lips smiled as he mused, while watching the splendors of a winter sunset. A soft rustle and the faint scent of violets warned him of Mrs. Snowdon's approach, and a sudden foreboding told him that danger was near. The instant he saw her face his fear was confirmed, for exultation, resolve, and love met and mingled in the expression it wore. Leaning in the window recess, where the red light shone full on her lovely face and queenly figure, she said, softly yet with a ruthless accent below the softness, "Dreaming dreams, Maurice, which will never come to pass, unless I will it. I know your secret, and I shall use it to prevent the fulfillment of the foolish hope you cherish."

"Who told you?" he demanded, with an almost fierce flash of the eye and an angry flush.

"I discovered it, as I warned you I should. My memory is good, I recall the gossip of long ago, I observe the faces, words, and acts of those whom I suspect, and unconscious hints from them give me the truth."

"I doubt it," and Treherne smiled securely.

She stooped and whispered one short sentence into his ear. Whatever it was it caused him to start up with a pale, panic-stricken face, and eye her as if she had pronounced his doom.

"Do you doubt it now?" she asked coldly.

"He told you! Even your skill and craft could not discover it alone," he muttered.

"Nay, I told you nothing was impossible to a determined woman. I needed no help, for I knew more than you think."

He sank down again in a despairing attitude and hid his face, saying mournfully, "I might have known you would hunt me down and dash my hopes when they were surest. How will you use this unhappy secret?"

"I will tell Octavia, and make her duty less hard. It will be kind to both of you, for even with her this memory would mar your happiness; and it saves her from the shame and grief of discovering, when too late, that she has given herself to a -"

"Stop!" he cried, in a tone that made her start and pale, as he rose out of his chair white with a stern indignation which awed her for a moment. "You shall not utter that word, you know but half the truth, and if you wrong me or trouble the girl I will turn traitor also, and tell the general the game you are playing with my cousin. You feign to love me as you feigned before, but his title is the bait now as then, and you fancy that by threatening to mar my hopes you will secure my silence, and gain your end."

"Wrong, quite wrong. Jasper is nothing to me; I use him as a tool, not you. If I threaten, it is to keep you from Octavia, who cannot forgive the past and love you for yourself, as I have done all these miserable months. You say I know but half the truth. Tell me the whole and I will spare you."

If ever a man was tempted to betray a trust it was Treherne then. A word, and Octavia might be his; silence, and she might be lost; for this woman was in earnest, and possessed the power to ruin his good name forever. The truth leaped to his lips and would have passed them, had not his eye fallen on the portrait of Jasper's father. This man had loved and sheltered the orphan all his life, had made of him a son, and, dying, urged him to guard and serve and save the rebellious youth he left, when most needing a father's care.

"I promised, and I will keep my promise at all costs," sighed Treherne, and with a gesture full of pathetic patience he waved the fair tempter from him, saying steadily, "I will never tell you, though you rob me of that which is dearer than my life. Go and work your will, but remember that when you might have won the deepest gratitude of the man you profess to love, you chose instead to earn his hatred and contempt."

Waiting for no word of hers, he took refuge in his room, and Edith Snowdon sank down upon the couch, struggling with contending emotions of love and jealousy, remorse and despair. How long she sat there she could not tell; an approaching step recalled her to herself, and looking up she saw Octavia. As the girl approached down the long vista of the drawing rooms, her youth and beauty, innocence and candor touched that fairer and more gifted woman with an envy she had never known before. Something in the girl's face struck her instantly: a look of peace and purity, a sweet serenity more winning than loveliness, more impressive than dignity or grace. With a smile on her lips, yet a half-sad, half-tender light in her eyes, and a cluster of pale winter roses in her hand, she came on till she stood before her rival and, offering the flowers, said, in words as simple as sincere, "Dear Mrs. Snowdon, I cannot let the last sun of the old year set on any misdeeds of mine for which I may atone. I have disliked, distrusted, and misjudged you, and now I come to you in all humility to say forgive me."

With the girlish abandon of her impulsive nature Octavia knelt down before the woman who was plotting to destroy her happiness, laid the roses like a little peace offering on her lap, and with eloquently pleading eyes waited for pardon. For a moment Mrs. Snowdon watched her, fancying it a well-acted ruse to disarm a dangerous rival; but in that sweet face there was no art; one glance showed her that. The words smote her to the heart and won her in spite of pride or passion, as she suddenly took the girl into her arms, weeping repentant tears. Neither spoke, but in the silence each felt the barrier which had stood between them vanishing, and each learned to know the other better in that moment than in a year of common life. Octavia rejoiced that the instinct which had prompted her to make this appeal had not misled her, but assured her that behind the veil of coldness, pride, and levity which this woman wore there was a heart aching for sympathy and help and love. Mrs. Snowdon felt her worser self slip from her, leaving all that was true and noble to make her worthy of the test applied. Art she could meet with equal art, but nature conquered her. For spite of her misspent life and faulty character, the germ of virtue, which lives in the worst, was there, only waiting for the fostering sun and dew of love to strengthen it, even though the harvest be a late one.

"Forgive you!" she cried, brokenly. "It is I who should ask forgiveness of you, I who should atone, confess, and repent. Pardon me, pity me, love me, for I am more wretched than you know."

"Dear, I do with heart and soul. Believe it, and let me be your friend" was the soft answer.

"God knows I need one!" sighed the poor woman, still holding fast the only creature who had wholly won her. "Child, I am not good, but not so bad that I dare not look in your innocent face and call you friend. I never had one of my own sex. I never knew my mother; and no one ever saw in me the possibility of goodness, truth, and justice but you. Trust and love and help me, Octavia, and I will reward you with a better life, if I can do no more."

"I will, and the new year shall be happier than the old."

"God bless you for that prophecy; may I be worthy of it."

Then as a bell warned them away, the rivals kissed each other tenderly, and parted friends. As Mrs. Snowdon entered her room, she saw her husband sitting with his gray head in his hands, and heard him murmur despairingly to himself, "My life makes her miserable. But for the sin of it I'd die to free her."

"No, live for me, and teach me to be happy in your love." The clear voice startled him, but not so much as the beautiful changed face of the wife who laid the gray head on her bosom, saying tenderly, "My kind and patient husband, you have been deceived. From me you shall know all the truth, and when you have forgiven my faulty past, you shall see how happy I will try to make your future."

Chapter VII

A Ghostly Revel

"Bless me, how dull we are tonight!" exclaimed Rose, as the younger portion of the party wandered listlessly about the drawing rooms that evening, while my lady and the major played an absorbing game of piquet, and the general dozed peacefully at last.

"It is because Maurice is not here; he always keeps us going, for he is a fellow of infinite resources," replied Sir Jasper, suppressing a yawn.

"Have him out then," said Annon.

"He won't come. The poor lad is blue tonight, in spite of his improvement. Something is amiss, and there is no getting a word from him."

"Sad memories afflict him, perhaps," sighed Blanche.

"Don't be absurd, dear, sad memories are all nonsense; melancholy is always indigestion, and nothing is so sure a cure as fun," said Rose briskly. "I'm going to send in a polite invitation begging him to come and amuse us. He'll accept, I haven't a doubt."

The message was sent, but to Rose's chagrin a polite refusal was returned.

"He shall come. Sir Jasper, do you and Mr. Annon go as a deputation from us, and return without him at your peril" was her command.

They went, and while waiting their reappearance the sisters spoke of what all had observed.

"How lovely Mrs. Snowdon looks tonight. I always thought she owed half her charms to her skill in dress, but she never looked so beautiful as in that plain black silk, with those roses in her hair," said Rose.

"What has she done to herself?" replied Blanche. "I see a change, but can't account for it. She and Tavie have made some beautifying discovery, for both look altogether uplifted and angelic all of a sudden."

"Here come the gentlemen, and, as I'm a Talbot, they haven't got him!" cried Rose as the deputation appeared, looking very crestfallen. "Don't come near me," she added, irefully, "you are disloyal cowards, and I doom you to exile till I want you. I am infinite in resources as well as this recreant man, and come he shall. Mrs. Snowdon, would you mind asking Mr. Treherne to suggest something to wile away the rest of this evening? We are in despair, and can think of nothing, and you are all-powerful with him."

"I must decline, since he refuses you" was the decided answer, as Mrs. Snowdon moved away.

"Tavie, dear, do go; we must have him; he always obeys you, and you would be such a public benefactor, you know."

Without a word Octavia wrote a line and sent it by a servant. Several minutes passed, and the gentlemen began to lay wagers on the success of her trial. "He will not come for me, you may be sure," said Octavia. As the words passed her lips he appeared.

A general laugh greeted him, but, taking no notice of the jests at his expense, he turned to Octavia, saying quietly, "What can I do for you, Cousin?"

His colorless face and weary eyes reproached her for disturbing him, but it was too late for regret, and she answered hastily, "We are in want of some new and amusing occupation to wile away the evening. Can you suggest something appropriate?"

"Why not sit round the hall fire and tell stories, while we wait to see the old year out, as we used to do long ago?" he asked, after a moment's thought.

"I told you so! There it is, just what we want." And Sir Jasper looked triumphant.

"It's capital, let us begin at once. It is after ten now, so we shall not have long to wait," cried Rose, and, taking Sir Jasper's arm, she led the way to the hall.

A great fire always burned there, and in wintertime thick carpets and curtains covered the stone floor and draped the tall windows. Plants blossomed in the warm atmosphere, and chairs and lounges stood about invitingly. The party was soon seated, and Treherne was desired to begin.

"We must have ghost stories, and in order to be properly thrilling and effective, the lights must be put out," said Rose, who sat next him, and spoke first, as usual.

This was soon done, and only a ruddy circle of firelight was left to oppose the rapt gloom that filled the hall, where shadows now seemed to lurk in every corner.

"Don't be very dreadful, or I shall faint away," pleaded Blanche, drawing nearer to Annon, for she had taken her sister's advice, and laid close siege to that gentleman's heart.

"I think your nerves will bear my little tale," replied Treherne. "When I was in India, four years ago, I had a very dear friend in my regiment, a Scotchman; I'm half Scotch myself, you know, and clannish, of course. Gordon was sent up the country on a scouting expedition, and never returned. His men reported that he left them one evening to take a survey, and his horse came home bloody and riderless. We searched, but could not find a trace of him, and I was desperate to discover and avenge his murder. About a month after his disappearance, as I sat in my tent one fearfully hot day, suddenly the canvas door flap was raised and there stood Gordon. I saw him as plainly as I see you, Jasper, and should have sprung to meet him, but something held me back. He was deathly pale, dripping with water, and in his bonny blue eyes was a wild, woeful look that made my blood run cold. I stared dumbly, for it was awful to see my friend so changed and so unearthly. Stretching his arm to me he took my hand, saying solemnly, 'Come!' The touch was like ice; an ominous thrill ran through me; I started up to obey, and he was gone."

"A horrid dream, of course. Is that all?" asked Rose.

With his eyes on the fire and his left hand half extended, Treherne went on as if he had not heard her.

"I thought it was a fancy, and soon recovered myself, for no one had seen or heard anything of Gordon, and my native servant lay just outside my tent. A strange sensation remained in the hand the phantom touched. It was cold, damp, and white. I found it vain to try to forget this apparition; it took strong hold of me; I told Yermid, my man, and he bade me consider it a sign that I was to seek my friend. That night I dreamed I was riding up the country in hot haste; what led me I know not, but I pressed on and on, longing to reach the end. A half-dried river crossed my path, and, riding down the steep bank to ford it, I saw Gordon's body lying in the shallow water looking exactly as the vision looked. I woke in a strange mood, told the story to my commanding officer, and, as nothing was doing just then, easily got leave of absence for a week. Taking Yermid, I set out on my sad quest. I thought it folly, but I could not resist the impulse that drew me on. For seven days I searched, and the strangest part of the story is that all that time I went on exactly as in the dream, seeing what I saw then, and led by the touch of a cold hand on mine. On the seventh day I reached the river, and found my friend's body."

"How horrible! Is it really true?" cried Mrs. Snowdon.

"As true as I am a living man. Nor is that all: this left hand of mine never has been warm since that time. See and feel for yourselves."

He opened both hands, and all satisfied themselves that the left was smaller, paler, and colder than the right.

"Pray someone tell another story to put this out of my mind; it makes me nervous," said Blanche.

"I'll tell one, and you may laugh to quiet your nerves. I want to have mine done with, so that I can enjoy the rest with a free mind." With these words Rose began her tale in the good old fashion.

"Once upon a time, when we were paying a visit to my blessed grandmamma, I saw a ghost in this wise: The dear old lady was ill with a cold and kept her room, leaving us to mope, for it was very dull in the great lonely house. Blanche and I were both homesick, but didn't like to leave till she was better, so we ransacked the library and solaced ourselves with all manner of queer books. One day I found Grandmamma very low and nervous, and evidently with something on her mind. She would say nothing, but the next day was worse, and I insisted on knowing the cause, for the trouble was evidently mental. Charging me to keep it from Blanche, who was, and is, a sad coward, she told me that a spirit had appeared to her two successive nights. 'If it comes a third time, I shall prepare to die,' said the foolish old lady.

"'No, you won't, for I'll come and stay with you and lay your ghost,' I said. With some difficulty I made her yield, and after Blanche was asleep I slipped away to Grandmamma, with a book and candle for a long watch, as the spirit didn't appear till after midnight. She usually slept with her door unlocked, in case of fire or fright, and her maid was close by. That night I locked the door, telling her that spirits could come through the oak if they chose, and I preferred to have a fair trial. Well, I read and chatted and dozed till dawn and nothing appeared, so I laughed at the whole affair, and the old lady pretended to be convinced that it was all a fancy.

"Next night I slept in my own room, and in the morning was told that not only Grandmamma but Janet had seen the spirit. All in white, with streaming hair, a pale face, and a red streak at the throat. It came and parted the bed-curtains, looking in a moment, and then vanished. Janet had slept with Grandmamma and kept a lamp burning on the chimney, so both saw it.

"I was puzzled, but not frightened; I never am, and I insisted on trying again. The door was left unlocked, as on the previous night, and I lay with Grandmamma, a light burning as before. About two she clutched me as I was dropping off. I looked, and there, peeping in between the dark curtains, was a pale face with long hair all about it, and a red streak at the throat. It was very dim, the light being low, but I saw it, and after one breathless minute sprang up, caught my foot, fell down with a crash, and by the time I was around the bed, not a vestige of the thing appeared. I was angry, and vowed I'd succeed at all hazards, though I'll confess I was just a bit daunted.

"Next time Janet and I sat up in easy chairs, with bright lights burning, and both wide awake with the strongest coffee we could make. As the hour drew near we got nervous, and when the white shape came gliding in Janet hid her face. I didn't, and after one look was on the point of laughing, for the spirit was Blanche walking in her sleep. She wore a coral necklace in those days, and never took it off, and her long hair half hid her face, which had the unnatural, uncanny look somnambulists always wear. I had the sense to keep still and tell Janet what to do, so the poor child went back unwaked, and Grandmamma's spirit never walked again for I took care of that."

"Why did you haunt the old lady?" asked Annon, as the laughter ceased.

"I don't know, unless it was that I wanted to ask leave to go home, and was afraid to do it awake, so tried when asleep. I shall not tell any story, as I was the heroine of this, but will give my turn to you, Mr. Annon," said Blanche, with a soft glance, which was quite thrown away, for the gentleman's eyes were fixed on Octavia, who sat on a low ottoman at Mrs. Snowdon's feet in the full glow of the firelight.

"I've had very small experience in ghosts, and can only recall a little fright I once had when a boy at college. I'd been out to a party, got home tired, couldn't find my matches, and retired in the dark. Toward morning I woke, and glancing up to see if the dim light was dawn or moonshine I was horrified to see a coffin standing at the bed's foot. I rubbed my eyes to be sure I was awake, and looked with all my might. There it was, a long black coffin, and I saw the white plate in the dusk, for the moon was setting and my curtain was not drawn. 'It's some trick of the fellows,' I thought; 'I'll not betray myself, but keep cool.' Easy to say but hard to do, for it suddenly flashed into my mind that I might be in the wrong room. I glanced about, but there were the familiar objects as usual, as far as the indistinct light allowed me to see, and I made sure by feeling on the wall at the bed's head for my watchcase. It was there, and mine beyond a doubt, being peculiar in shape and fabric. Had I been to a college wine party I could have accounted for the vision, but a quiet evening in a grave professor's well-conducted family could produce no ill effects. 'It's an optical illusion, or a prank of my mates; I'll sleep and forget it,' I said, and for a time endeavored to do so, but curiosity overcame my resolve, and soon I peeped again. Judge of my horror when I saw the sharp white outline of a dead face, which seemed to be peeping up from the coffin. It gave me a terrible shock for I was but a lad and had been ill. I hid my face and quaked like a nervous girl, still thinking it some joke and too proud to betray fear lest I should be laughed at. How long I lay there I don't know, but when I looked again the face was farther out and the whole figure seemed rising slowly. The moon was nearly down, I had no lamp, and to be left in the dark with that awesome thing was more than I could bear. Joke or earnest, I must end the panic, and bolting out of my room I roused my neighbor. He told me I was mad or drunk, but lit a lamp and returned with me, to find my horror only a heap of clothes thrown on the table in such a way that, as the moon's pale light shot it, it struck upon my black student's gown, with a white card lying on it, and produced the effect of a coffin and plate. The face was a crumpled handkerchief, and what seemed hair a brown muffler. As the moon sank, these outlines changed and, incredible as it may seem, grew like a face. My friend not having had the fright enjoyed the joke, and 'Coffins' was my sobriquet for a long while."

"You get worse and worse. Sir Jasper, do vary the horrors by a touch of fun, or I shall run away," said Blanche, glancing over her shoulder nervously.

"I'll do my best, and tell a story my uncle used to relate of his young days. I forget the name of the place, but it was some little country town famous among anglers. My uncle often went to fish, and always regretted that a deserted house near the trout stream was not occupied, for the inn was inconveniently distant. Speaking of this one evening as he lounged in the landlady's parlor, he asked why no one took it and let the rooms to strangers in the fishing season. 'For fear of the ghostissess, your honor,' replied the woman, and proceeded to tell, him that three distinct spirits haunted the house. In the garret was heard the hum of a wheel and the tap of high-heeled shoes, as the ghostly spinner went to and fro. In a chamber sounded the sharpening of a knife, followed by groans and the drip of blood. The cellar was made awful by a skeleton sitting on a half-buried box and chuckling fiendishly. It seems a miser lived there once, and was believed to have starved his daughter in the garret, keeping her at work till she died. The second spirit was that of the girl's rejected lover, who cut his throat in the chamber, and the third of the miser who was found dead on the money chest he was too feeble to conceal. My uncle laughed at all this, and offered to lay the ghosts if anyone would take the house.

"This offer got abroad, and a crusty old fellow accepted it, hoping to turn a penny. He had a pretty girl, whose love had been thwarted by the old man, and whose lover was going to sea in despair. My uncle knew this and pitied the young people. He had made acquaintance with a wandering artist, and the two agreed to conquer the prejudices against the house by taking rooms there. They did so, and after satisfying themselves regarding the noises, consulted a wise old woman as to the best means of laying the ghosts. She told them if any young girl would pass a night in each haunted room, praying piously the while, that all would be well. Peggy was asked if she would do it, and being a stouthearted lass she consented, for a round sum, to try it. The first night was in the garret, and Peggy, in spite of the prophecies of the village gossips, came out alive, though listeners at the door heard the weird humming and tapping all night long. The next night all went well, and from that time no more sharpening, groaning, or dripping was heard. The third time she bade her friends good-bye and, wrapped in her red cloak, with a lamp and prayer book, went down into the cellar. Alas for pretty Peggy! When day came she was gone, and with her the miser's empty box, though his bones remained to prove how well she had done her work.

"The town was in an uproar, and the old man furious. Some said the devil had flown away with her, others that the bones were hers, and all agreed that henceforth another ghost would haunt the house. My uncle and the artist did their best to comfort the father, who sorely reproached himself for thwarting the girl's love, and declared that if Jack would find her he should have her. But Jack had sailed, and the old man 'was left lamenting.' The house was freed from its unearthly visitors, however, for no ghost appeared; and when my uncle left, old Martin found money and letter informing him that Peggy had spent her first two nights preparing for flight, and on the third had gone away to marry and sail with Jack. The noises had been produced by the artist, who was a ventriloquist, the skeleton had been smuggled from the surgeons, and the whole thing was a conspiracy to help Peggy and accommodate the fishermen."

"It is evident that roguery is hereditary," laughed Rose as the narrator paused.

"I strongly suspect that Sir Jasper the second was the true hero of that story," added Mrs. Snowdon.

"Think what you like, I've done my part, and leave the stage for you, madam."

"I will come last. It is your turn, dear." As Mrs. Snowdon softly uttered the last word, and Octavia leaned upon her knee with an affectionate glance, Treherne leaned forward to catch a glimpse of the two changed faces, and looked as if bewildered when both smiled at him, as they sat hand in hand while the girl told her story.

"Long ago a famous actress suddenly dropped dead at the close of a splendidly played tragedy. She was carried home, and preparations were made to bury her. The play had been gotten up with great care and expense, and a fine actor was the hero. The public demanded a repetition, and an inferior person was engaged to take the dead lady's part. A day's delay had been necessary, but when the night came the house was crowded. They waited both before and behind the curtain for the debut of the new actress, with much curiosity. She stood waiting for her cue, but as it was given, to the amazement of all, the great tragedienne glided upon the stage. Pale as marble, and with a strange fire in her eyes, strange pathos in her voice, strange power in her acting, she went through her part, and at the close vanished as mysteriously as she came. Great was the excitement that night, and intense the astonishment and horror next day when it was whispered abroad that the dead woman never had revived, but had lain in her coffin before the eyes of watchers all the evening, when hundreds fancied they were applauding her at the theater. The mystery never was cleared up, and Paris was divided by two opinions: one that some person marvelously like Madame Z. had personated her for the sake of a sensation; the other that the ghost of the dead actress, unable to free itself from the old duties so full of fascination to an ambitious and successful woman, had played for the last time the part which had made her famous."

"Where did you find that, Tavie? It's very French, and not bad if you invented it," said Sir Jasper.

"I read it in an old book, where it was much better told. Now, Edith, there is just time for your tale."

As the word "Edith" passed her lips, again Treherne started and eyed them both, and again they smiled, as Mrs. Snowdon caressed the smooth cheek leaning on her knee, and looking full at him began the last recital.

"You have been recounting the pranks of imaginary ghosts; let me show you the workings of some real spirits, evil and good, that haunt every heart and home, making its misery or joy. At Christmastime, in a country house, a party of friends met to keep the holidays, and very happily they might have done so had not one person marred the peace of several. Love, jealousy, deceit, and nobleness were the spirits that played their freaks with these people. The person of whom I speak was more haunted than the rest, and much tormented, being willful, proud, and jealous. Heaven help her, she had had no one to exorcise these ghosts for her, and they goaded her to do much harm. Among these friends there were more than one pair of lovers, and much tangling of plots and plans, for hearts are wayward and mysterious things, and cannot love as duty bids or prudence counsels. This woman held the key to all the secrets of the house, and, having a purpose to gain, she used her power selfishly, for a time. To satisfy a doubt, she feigned a fancy for a gentleman who once did her the honor of admiring her, and, to the great scandal of certain sage persons, permitted him to show his regard for her, knowing that it was but a transient amusement on his part as well as upon hers. In the hands of this woman lay a secret which could make or mar the happiness of the best and dearest of the party. The evil spirits which haunted her urged her to mar their peace and gratify a sinful hope. On the other side, honor, justice, and generosity prompted her to make them happy, and while she wavered there came to her a sweet enchantress who, with a word, banished the tormenting ghosts forever, and gave the haunted woman a talisman to keep her free henceforth."

There the earnest voice faltered, and with a sudden impulse Mrs. Snowdon bent her head and kissed the fair forehead which had bent lower and lower as she went on. Each listener understood the truth, lightly veiled in that hasty fable, and each found in it a different meaning. Sir Jasper frowned and bit his lips, Annon glanced anxiously from face to face, Octavia hid hers, and Treherne's flashed with sudden intelligence, while Rose laughed low to herself, enjoying the scene. Blanche, who was getting sleepy, said, with a stifled gape, "That is a very nice, moral little story, but I wish there had been some real ghosts in it."

"There was. Will you come and see them?"

As she put the question, Mrs. Snowdon rose abruptly, wishing to end the séance, and beckoning them to follow glided up the great stairway. All obeyed, wondering what whim possessed her, and quite ready for any jest in store for them.

Chapter VIII

Jasper

She led them to the north gallery and, pausing at the door, said merrily, "The ghost, or ghosts rather, for there were two, which frightened Patty were Sir Jasper and myself, meeting to discuss certain important matters which concerned Mr. Treherne. If you want to see spirits we will play phantom for you, and convince you of our power."

"Good, let us go and have a ghostly dance, as a proper finale of our revel," answered Rose as they flocked into the long hall.

At that moment the great clock struck twelve, and all paused to bid the old year adieu. Sir Jasper was the first to speak, for, angry with Mrs. Snowdon, yet thankful to her for making a jest to others of what had been earnest to him, he desired to hide his chagrin under a gay manner; and taking Rose around the waist was about to waltz away as she proposed, saying cheerily, "'Come one and all, and dance the new year in,'" when a cry from Octavia arrested him, and turning he saw her stand, pale and trembling, pointing to the far end of the hall.

Eight narrow Gothic windows pierced either wall of the north gallery. A full moon sent her silvery light strongly in upon the eastern side, making broad bars of brightness across the floor. No fires burned there now, and wherever the moonlight did not fall deep shadows lay. As Octavia cried out, all looked, and all distinctly saw a tall, dark figure moving noiselessly across the second bar of light far down the hall.

"Is it some jest of yours?" asked Sir Jasper of Mrs. Snowdon, as the form vanished in the shadow.

"No, upon my honor, I know nothing of it! I only meant to relieve Octavia's superstitious fears by showing her our pranks" was the whispered reply as Mrs. Snowdon's cheek paled, and she drew nearer to Jasper.

"Who is there?" called Treherne in a commanding tone.

No answer, but a faint, cold breath of air seemed to sigh along the arched roof and die away as the dark figure crossed the third streak of moonlight. A strange awe fell upon them all, and no one spoke, but stood watching for the appearance of the shape. Nearer and nearer it came, with soundless steps, and as it reached the sixth window its outlines were distinctly visible. A tall, wasted figure, all in black, with a rosary hanging from the girdle, and a dark beard half concealing the face.

"The Abbot's ghost, and very well got up," said Annon, trying to laugh but failing decidedly, for again the cold breath swept over them, causing a general shudder.

"Hush!" whispered Treherne, drawing Octavia to his side with a protecting gesture.

Once more the phantom appeared and disappeared, and as they waited for it to cross the last bar of light that lay between it and them, Mrs. Snowdon stepped forward to the edge of the shadow in which they stood, as if to confront the apparition alone. Out of the darkness it came, and in the full radiance of the light it paused. Mrs. Snowdon, being nearest, saw the face first, and uttering a faint cry dropped down upon the stone floor, covering up her eyes. Nothing human ever wore a look like that of the ghastly, hollow-eyed, pale-lipped countenance below the hood. All saw it and held their breath as it slowly raised a shadowy arm and pointed a shriveled finger at Sir Jasper.

"Speak, whatever you are, or I'll quickly prove whether you are man or spirit!" cried Jasper fiercely, stepping forward as if to grasp the extended arm that seemed to menace him alone.

An icy gust swept through the hall, and the phantom slowly receded into the shadow. Jasper sprang after it, but nothing crossed the second stream of light, and nothing remained in the shade. Like one possessed by a sudden fancy he rushed down the gallery to find all fast and empty, and to return looking very strangely. Blanche had fainted away and Annon was bearing her out of the hall. Rose was clinging to Mrs. Snowdon, and Octavia leaned against her cousin, saying in a fervent whisper, "Thank God it did not point at you!"

"Am I then dearer than your brother?" he whispered back.

There was no audible reply, but one little hand involuntarily pressed his, though the other was outstretched toward Jasper, who came up white and startled but firm and quiet. Affecting to make light of it, he said, forcing a smile as he raised Mrs. Snowdon, "It is some stupid joke of the servants. Let us think no more of it. Come, Edith, this is not like your usual self."

"It was nothing human, Jasper; you know it as well as I. Oh, why did I bring you here to meet the warning phantom that haunts your house!"

"Nay, if my time is near the spirit would have found me out wherever I might be. I have no faith in that absurd superstition; I laugh at and defy it. Come down and drink my health in wine from the Abbot's own cellar."

But no one had heart for further gaiety, and, finding Lady Treherne already alarmed by Annon, they were forced to tell her all, and find their own bewilderment deepened by her unalterable belief in the evil omen.

At her command the house was searched, the servants cross-questioned, and every effort made to discover the identity of the apparition. All in vain; the house was as usual, and not a man or maid but turned pale at the idea of entering the gallery at midnight. At my lady's request, all promised to say no more upon the mystery, and separated at last to such sleep as they could enjoy.

Very grave were the faces gathered about the breakfast table next morning, and very anxious the glances cast on Sir Jasper as he came in, late as usual, looking uncommonly blithe and well. Nothing serious ever made a deep impression on his mercurial nature. Treherne had more the air of a doomed man, being very pale and worn, in spite of an occasional gleam of happiness as he looked at Octavia. He haunted Jasper like a shadow all the morning, much to that young gentleman's annoyance, for both his mother and sister hung about him with faces of ill-dissembled anxiety. By afternoon his patience gave out, and he openly rebelled against the tender guard kept over him. Ringing for his horse he said decidedly, "I'm bored to death with the solemnity which pervades the house today, so I'm off for a brisk gallop, before I lose my temper and spirits altogether."

"Come with me in the pony carriage, Jasper. I've not had a drive with you for a long while, and should enjoy it so much," said my lady, detaining him.

"Mrs. Snowdon looks as if she needed air to revive her roses, and the pony carriage is just the thing for her, so I will cheerfully resign my seat to her," he answered laughing, as he forced himself from his mother's hand.

"Take the girls in the clarence. We all want a breath of air, and you are the best whip we know. Be gallant and say yes, dear."

"No, thank you, Tavie, that won't do. Rose and Blanche are both asleep, and you are dying to go and do likewise, after your vigils last night. As a man and a brother I beg you'll do so, and let me ride as I like."

"Suppose you ask Annon to join you -" began Treherne with well-assumed indifference; but Sir Jasper frowned and turned sharply on him, saying, half-petulantly, half-jocosely:

"Upon my life I should think I was a boy or a baby, by the manner in which you mount guard over me today. If you think I'm going to live in daily fear of some mishap, you are all much mistaken. Ghost or no ghost, I shall make merry while I can; a short life and a jolly one has always been my motto, you know, so fare you well till dinnertime."

They watched him gallop down the avenue, and then went their different ways, still burdened with a nameless foreboding. Octavia strolled into the conservatory, thinking to refresh herself with the balmy silence which pervaded the place, but Annon soon joined her, full of a lover's hopes and fears.

"Miss Treherne, I have ventured to come for my answer. Is my New Year to be a blissful or a sad one?" he asked eagerly.

"Forgive me if I give you an unwelcome reply, but I must be true, and so regretfully refuse the honor you do me," she said sorrowfully.

"May I ask why?"

"Because I do not love you."

"And you do love your cousin," he cried angrily, pausing to watch her half-averted face.

She turned it fully toward him and answered, with her native sincerity, "Yes, I do, with all my heart, and now my mother will not thwart me, for Maurice has saved my life, and I am free to devote it all to him."

"Happy man, I wish I had been a cripple!" sighed Annon. Then with a manful effort to be just and generous, he added heartily, "Say no more, he deserves you; I want no sacrifice to duty; I yield, and go away, praying heaven to bless you now and always."

He kissed her hand and left her to seek my lady and make his adieus, for no persuasion could keep him. Leaving a note for Sir Jasper, he hurried away, to the great relief of Treherne and the deep regret of Blanche, who, however, lived in hopes of another trial later in the season.

"Here comes Jasper, Mamma, safe and well," cried Octavia an hour or two later, as she joined her mother on the terrace, where my lady had been pacing restlessly to and fro nearly ever since her son rode away.

With a smile of intense relief she waved her handkerchief as he came clattering up the drive, and seeing her he answered with hat and hand. He usually dismounted at the great hall door, but a sudden whim made him ride along the wall that lay below the terrace, for he was a fine horseman, and Mrs. Snowdon was looking from her window. As he approached, the peacocks fled screaming, and one flew up just before the horse's eyes as his master was in the act of dismounting. The spirited creature was startled, sprang partway up the low, broad steps of the terrace, and, being sharply checked, slipped, fell, and man and horse rolled down together.

Never did those who heard it forget the cry that left Lady Treherne's lips as she saw the fall. It brought out both guests and servants, to find Octavia recklessly struggling with the frightened horse, and my lady down upon the stones with her son's bleeding head in her arms.

They bore in the senseless, shattered body, and for hours tried everything that skill and sciences could devise to save the young man's life. But every effort was in vain, and as the sun set Sir Jasper lay dying. Conscious at last, and able to speak, he looked about him with a troubled glance, and seemed struggling with some desire that overmastered pain and held death at bay.

"I want Maurice," he feebly said, at length.

"Dear lad, I'm here," answered his cousin's voice from a seat in the shadow of the half-drawn curtains.

"Always near when I need you. Many a scrape have you helped me out of, but this is beyond your power," and a faint smile passed over Jasper's lips as the past flitted before his mind. But the smile died, and a groan of pain escaped him as he cried suddenly, "Quick! Let me tell it before it is too late! Maurice never will, but bear the shame all his life that my dead name may be untarnished. Bring Edith; she must hear the truth."

She was soon there, and, lying in his mother's arms, one hand in his cousin's, and one on his sister's bent head, Jasper rapidly told the secret which had burdened him for a year.

"I did it; I forged my uncle's name when I had lost so heavily at play that I dared not tell my mother, or squander more of my own fortune. I deceived Maurice, and let him think the check a genuine one; I made him present it and get the money, and when all went well I fancied I was safe. But my uncle discovered it secretly, said nothing, and, believing Maurice the forger, disinherited him. I never knew this till the old man died, and then it was too late. I confessed to Maurice, and he forgave me. He said, 'I am helpless now, shut out from the world, with nothing to lose or gain, and soon to be forgotten by those who once knew me, so let the suspicion of shame, if any such there be, still cling to me, and do you go your way, rich, happy, honorable, and untouched by any shadow on your fame.' Mother, I let him do it, unconscious as he was that many knew the secret sin and fancied him the doer of it."

"Hush, Jasper, let it pass. I can bear it; I promised your dear father to be your staunch friend through life, and I have only kept my word."

"God knows you have, but now my life ends, and I cannot die till you are cleared. Edith, I told you half the truth, and you would have used it against him had not some angel sent this girl to touch your heart. You have done your part to atone for the past, now let me do mine. Mother, Tavie loves him, he has risked life and honor for me. Repay him generously and give him this."

With feeble touch Sir Jasper tried to lay his sister's hand in Treherne's as he spoke; Mrs. Snowdon helped him, and as my lady bowed her head in silent acquiescence, a joyful smile shone on the dying man's face.

"One more confession, and then I am ready," he said, looking up into the face of the woman whom he had loved with all the power of a shallow nature. "It was a jest to you, Edith, but it was bitter earnest to me, for I loved you, sinful as it was. Ask your husband to forgive me, and tell him it was better I should die than live to mar a good man's peace. Kiss me once, and make him happy for my sake."

She touched his cold lips with remorseful tenderness, and in the same breath registered a vow to obey that dying prayer.

"Tavie dear, Maurice, my brother, God bless you both. Good-bye, Mother. He will be a better son than I have been to you." Then, the reckless spirit of the man surviving to the last, Sir Jasper laughed faintly, as he seemed to beckon some invisible shape, and died saying gaily, "Now, Father Abbot, lead on, I'll follow you."

A year later three weddings were celebrated on the same day and in the same church. Maurice Treherne, a well man, led up his cousin. Frank Annon rewarded Blanche's patient siege by an unconditional surrender, and, to the infinite amusement of Mrs. Grundy, Major Royston publicly confessed himself outgeneraled by merry Rose. The triple wedding feast was celebrated at Treherne Abbey, and no uncanny visitor marred its festivities, for never again was the north gallery haunted by the ghostly Abbot.

Becky's Christmas Dream

All alone by the kitchen fire, sat little Becky, for every one else had gone away to keep Christmas and left her to take care of the house. Nobody had thought to give her any presents, or take her to any merrymaking, or remembered that Christmas should be made a happy time to every child, whether poor or rich.

She was only twelve years old, this little girl from the poorhouse, who was bound to work for the farmer's wife till she was eighteen. She had no father or mother, no friends or home but this, and as she sat alone by the fire her little heart ached for some one to love and cherish her.

Becky was a shy, quiet child, with a thin face and wistful eyes that always seemed trying to find something that she wanted very much. She worked away, day after day, so patiently and silently that no one ever guessed what curious thoughts filled the little cropped head, or what a tender child's heart was hidden under the blue checked pinafore.

To-night she was wishing that there were fairies in the world, who would whisk down the chimney and give her quantities of pretty things, as they did in the delightful fairy tales.

"I'm sure I am as poor and lonely as Cinderella, and need a kind godmother to help me as much as ever she did," said Becky to herself. She sat on her little stool staring at the fire, which didn't burn very well, for she felt too much out of sorts to care whether things looked cheerful or not.

There is an old belief that all dumb things can speak for one hour on Christmas Eve. Now, Becky knew nothing of this story and no one can say whether what happened was true or whether she fell asleep and dreamed it. But certain it is when Becky compared herself to Cinderella, she was amazed to hear a small voice: reply, "Well, my dear, if you want advice, I shall be very glad to give you some, for I've had much experience in this trying world.

Becky stared about her, but all she saw was the old gray cat, blinking at the fire.

"Did you speak, Tabby?" said the child, at last.

"Of course I did. If you wish a godmother, here I am."

Becky laughed at the idea; but Puss, with her silver-gray suit, white handkerchief crossed on her bosom, kind, motherly old face, and cosy purr, did make a very good Quakerish little godmother after all.

"Well, ma'am, I'm ready to listen," said Becky respectfully.

"First, my child, what do you want most?" asked the godmother, quite in the fairy-book style.

"To be loved by everybody," answered Becky.

"Good!" said the cat. "I'm pleased with that answer, it's sensible, and I'll tell you how to get your wish. Learn to make people love you by loving them."

"I don't know how," sighed Becky.

"No more did I in the beginning," returned Puss. "When I first came here, a shy young kitten, I thought only of keeping out of everybody's way, for I was afraid of every one. I hid under the barn and only came out when no one was near. I wasn't happy, for I wanted to be petted, but didn't know how to begin. One day I heard Aunt Sally say to the master, 'James, that wild kitten isn't any use at all, you had better drown her and get a nice tame one to amuse the children and clear the house of mice.' 'The poor thing has been abused, I guess, so we will give her another trial and may be she will come to trust us after a while,' said the good master. I thought over these things as I lay under the barn and resolved to do my best, for I did not want to be drowned. It was hard at first, but I began by coming out when little Jane called me and letting her play with me. Then I ventured into the house, and finding a welcome at my first visit, I went again and took a mouse with me to show that I wasn't idle. No one hurt or frightened me and soon I was the household pet. For several years I have led a happy life here."

Becky listened eagerly and when Puss had ended, she said timidly, "Do you think if I try not to be afraid, but to show that I want to be affectionate, the people will let me and will like it?"

"Very sure. I heard the mistress say you were a good, handy little thing. Do as I did, my dear, and you will find that there is plenty of love in the world."

"I will. Thank y u, dear old Puss, for your advice."

Puss came to rub her soft cheek against Becky's hand, and then settled herself in a cosy hunch in Becky's lap. Presently another voice spoke, a queer, monotonous voice, high above her.

"Tick, tick; wish again, little Becky, and I'll tell you how to find your wish."

It was the old moon-faced clock behind the door, which had struck twelve just before Tabby first spoke.

"Dear me," said Becky, "how queerly things do act to-night!" She thought a moment then said soberly, "I wish I liked my work better. Washing dishes, picking chips and hemming towels is such tiresome work, I don't see how I can go on doing it for six more years."

"Just what I used to feel," said the clock. "I couldn't bear to think that I had got to stand here and do nothing but tick year after year. I flatly said I wouldn't, and I stopped a dozen times a day. Bless me, what a fuss I made until I was put in this corner to stand idle for several months. At first I rejoiced, then I got tired of doing nothing and began to reflect that as I was born a clock, it would be wiser to do my duty and get some satisfaction out of it if I could."

"And so you went to going again? Please teach me to be faithful and to love my duty," cried Becky.

"I will;" and the old clock grandly struck the half hour, with a smile on its round face, as it steadily ticked on.

Here the fire blazed up and the tea-kettle hanging on the crane began to sing.

"How cheerful that is!" said Becky, as the whole kitchen brightened with the ruddy glow. "If I could have a third wish, I'd wish to be as cheerful as the fire."

"Have your wish if you choose, but you must work for it, as I do," cried the fire, as its flames embraced the old kettle till it gurgled with pleasure.

Becky thought she heard a queer voice humming these words

"I'm an old black kettle,
With a very crooked nose.
But I can't help being gay
When the jolly fire glows."

"I shouldn't wonder a mite if that child had been up to mischief to-night, rummaged all over the house, eaten herself sick, or stolen something and run away with it," fretted Aunt Sally, as the family went jingling home in the big sleigh about one o'clock from the Christmas party.

"Tut, tut, Aunty, I wouldn't think evil of the poor little thing. If I'd had my way she would have gone with us and had a good time. She doesn't look as if she had seen many, and I have a notion it is what she needs," said the farmer kindly.

"The thought of her alone at home has worried me all the evening, but she didn't seem to mind, and I haven't had time to get a respectable dress ready for her to wear, so I let it go," added the farmer's wife, as she cuddled little Jane under the cloaks and shawls, with a regretful memory of Becky knocking at her heart.

"I've got some pop corn and a bouncing big apple for her," said Billy, the red-faced lad perched up by his father playing drive.

"And I'll give her one of my dolls. She said she never had one, wasn't that dreadful?" put in little Jane, popping out her head like a bird from its nest.

"Better see what she has been doing first, advised Aunt Sally. "If she hasn't done any mischief and has remembered to have the kettle boiling so I can have a cup of hot tea after my ride, and if she has kept the fire up and warmed my slippers, I don't know but I'll give her the red mittens I knit."

They found poor Becky lying on the bare floor, her head pillowed on the stool, and old Tabby in her arms, with a corner of the blue pinafore spread over her. The fire was burning splendidly, the kettle simmering, and in a row upon the hearth stood, not only Aunt Sally's old slippers, but those of master and mistress also, and over a chair hung two little nightgowns warming for the children.

'Well now, who could have been more thoughtful than that!" said Aunt Sally. "Becky shall have those mittens, and I'll knit her two pairs of stockings, that I will."

So Aunt Sally laid the gay mittens close to the little rough hand that had worked so busily all day. Billy set his big red apple and bag of pop corn just where she would see them when she woke. Jane laid the doll in Becky's arms, and Tabby smelt of it approvingly, to the children's delight. The farmer had no present ready, but he stroked the little cropped head with a fatherly touch that made Becky smile in her sleep, as he said within himself, "I will do by this forlorn child as I would wish any one to do by my Janey if she were left alone." But the mother gave the best gift of all, for she stooped down and kissed Becky as only mothers can kiss. The good woman's heart reproached her for neglect of the child who had no mother.

That unusual touch wakened Becky at once, and looking about her with astonished eyes, she saw such a wonderful change in all the faces, that she clapped her hands and cried with a happy laugh, "My dream's come true! Oh, my dream's come true !"

Tilly's Christmas

"I'm so glad to-morrow is Christmas, because I'm going to have lots of presents."

"So am I glad, though I don't expect any presents but a pair of mittens."

"And so am I ; but I shan't have any presents at all."

As the three little girls trudged home from school they said these things, and as Tilly spoke, both the others looked at her with pity and some surprise, for she spoke cheerfully, and they wondered how she could be happy when she was so poor she could have no presents on Christmas.

"Don't you wish you could find a purse full of money right here in the path?" said Kate, the child who was going to have " lots of presents." "

"Oh, don't I, if I could keep it honestly!" and Tilly's eyes shone at the very thought.

"What would you buy?" asked Bessy, rubbing her cold hands, and longing for her mittens.

"I'd buy a pair of large, warm blankets, a load of wood, a shawl for mother, and a pair of shoes for me ; and if there was enough left, I'd give Bessy a new hat, and then she needn't wear Ben's old felt one," answered Tilly.

The girls laughed at that; but Bessy pulled the funny hat over her ears, and said she was much obliged, but she'd rather have candy.

"Let's look, and may be we can find a purse. People are always going about with money at Christmas time, and some one may lose it here," said Kate.

So, as they went along the snowy road, they looked about them, half in earnest, half in fun. Suddenly Tilly sprang forward, exclaiming,

"I see it! I've found it!"

The others followed, but all stopped disappointed; for it wasn't a purse, it was only a little bird. It lay upon the snow with its wings spread and feebly fluttering, as if too weak to fly. Its little feet were benumbed with cold; its once bright eyes were dull with pain, and instead of a blithe song, it could only utter a faint chirp, now and then, as if crying for help.

"Nothing but a stupid old robin; how provoking! " cried Kate, sitting down to rest.

"I shan't touch it. I found one once, and took care of it, and the ungrateful thing flew away the minute it was well," said Bessy, creeping under Kate's shawl, and putting her hands under her chin to warm them.

"Poor little birdie! How pitiful he looks, and how glad he must be to see some one coming to help him! I'll take him up gently, and carry him home to mother. Don't be frightened, dear, I'm your friend;" and Tilly knelt down in the snow, stretching her hand to the bird with the tenderest pity in her face.

Kate and Bessy laughed.

"Don't stop for that thing; it's getting late and cold: let's go on and look for the purse," they said, moving away.

"You wouldn't leave it to die?' cried Tilly.

"I'd rather have the bird than the money, so I shan't look any more. The purse wouldn't be mine, and I should only be tempted to keep it; but this poor thing will thank and love me, and I'm so glad I came in time."

Gently lifting the bird, Tilly felt its tiny cold claws cling to her hand, and saw its dim eyes brighten as it nestled down with a grateful chirp.

"Now I've got a Christmas present after all," she said, smiling, as they walked on. "I always wanted a bird, and this one will be such a pretty pet for me!"

"He'll fly away the first chance he gets, and die anyhow; so you'd better not waste your time over him," said Bessy.

"He can't pay you for taking care of him, and my mother says it isn't worth while to help folks that can't help us," added Kate.

"My mother says, ' Do as you'd be done by;' and I'm sure I'd like any one to help me if I was dying of cold and hunger.' Love your neighbor as yourself? is another of her sayings. This bird is my little neighbor, and I'll love him and care for him, as I often wish our rich neighbor would love and care for us," answered Tilly, breathing her warm breath over the benumbed bird, who looked up at her with confiding eyes, quick to feel and know a friend.

"What a funny girl you are," said Kate; "caring for that silly bird, and talking about loving your neighbor in that sober way. Mr. King don't care a bit for you, and never will, though he knows how poor you are; so I don't think your plan amounts to much."

"I believe it, though; and shall do my part, any way. Good-night. I hope you'll have a merry Christmas, and lots of pretty things," answered Tilly, as they parted.

Her eyes were full, and she felt so poor as she went on alone toward the little old house where she lived. It would have been so pleasant to know that she was going to have some of the pretty things all children love to find in their full stockings on Christmas morning. And pleasanter still to have been able to give her mother something nice. So many comforts were needed, and there was no hope of getting them; for they could barely get food and fire.

"Never mind, birdie, we'll make the best of what we have, and be merry in spite of every thing. You shall have a happy Christmas, any way; and I know God won't forget us, if every one else does."

She stopped a minute to wipe her eyes, and lean her cheek against the bird's soft breast, finding great comfort in the little creature, though it could only love her, nothing more.

"See, mother, what a nice present I've found," she cried, going in with a cheery face that was like sunshine in the dark room.

"I'm glad of that, dearie; for I haven't been able to get my little girl any thing but a rosy apple. Poor bird! Give it some of your warm bread and milk."

"Why, mother, what a big bowlful! I'm afraid you gave me all the milk," said Tilly, smiling over the nice, steaming supper that stood ready for her.

"I've had plenty, dear. Sit down and dry your wet feet, and put the bird in my basket on this warm flannel."

Tilly peeped into the closet and saw nothing there but dry bread.

"Mother's given me all the milk, and is going without her tea, 'cause she knows I'm hungry. Now I'll surprise her, and she shall have a good supper too. She is going to split wood, and I'll fix it while she's gone."

So Tilly put down the old tea-pot, carefully poured out a part of the milk, and from her pocket produced a great, plummy bun, that one of the school-children had given her, and she had saved for her mother. A slice of the dry bread was nicely toasted, and the bit of butter set by for her put on it. When her mother came in there was the table drawn up in a warm place, a hot cup of tea ready, and Tilly and birdie waiting for her.

Such a poor little supper, and yet such a happy one ; for love, charity, and contentment were guests there, and that Christmas eve was a blither one than that up at the great house, where lights shone, fires blazed, a great tree glittered, and music sounded, as the children danced and played.

"We must go to bed early, for we've only wood enough to last over to-morrow. I shall be paid for my work the day after, and then we can get some," said Tilly's mother, as they sat by the fire.

"If my bird was only a fairy bird, and would give us three wishes, how nice it would be! Poor dear, he can't give me any thing; but it's no matter," answered Tilly, looking at the robin, who lay in the basket with his head under his wing, a mere little feathery bunch.

"He can give you one thing, Tilly, the pleasure of doing good. That is one of the sweetest things in life; and the poor can enjoy it as well as the rich."

As her mother spoke, with her tired hand softly stroking her little daughter's hair, Tilly suddenly started and pointed to the window, saying, in a frightened whisper,

"I saw a face, a man's face, looking in! It's gone now; but I truly saw it."

"Some traveller attracted by the light perhaps. I'll go and see." And Tilly's mother went to the door.

No one was there. The wind blew cold, the stars shone, the snow lay white on field and wood, and the Christmas moon was glittering in the sky.

"What sort of a face was it?" asked Tilly's mother, coming back.

"A pleasant sort of face, I think ; but I was so startled I don't quite know what it was like. I wish we had a curtain there," said Tilly.

"I like to have our light shine out in the evening, for the road is dark and lonely just here, and the twinkle of our lamp is pleasant to people's eyes as they go by. We can do so little for our neighbors, I am glad to cheer the way for them. Now put these poor old shoes to dry, and go to bed, dearie; I'll come soon."

Tilly went, taking her bird with her to sleep in his basket near by, lest he should be lonely in the night.

Soon the little house was dark and still, and no one saw the Christmas spirits at their work that night.

When Tilly opened the door next morning, she gave a loud cry, clapped her hands, and then stood still, quite speechless with wonder and delight. There, before the door, lay a great pile of wood, all ready to burn, a big bundle and a basket; with a lovely nosegay of winter roses, holly, and evergreen tied to the handle.

"Oh, mother! did the fairies do it?" cried Tilly, pale with her happiness, as she seized the basket, while her mother took in the bundle.

"Yes, dear, the best and dearest fairy in the world, called ' Charity. ' She walks abroad at Christmas time, does beautiful deeds like this, and does not stay to be thanked," answered her mother with full eyes, as she undid the parcel.

There they were, the warm, thick blankets, the comfortable shawl, the new shoes, and, best of all, a pretty winter hat for Bessy. The basket was full of good things to eat, and on the flowers lay a paper saying,

"For the little girl who loves her neighbor as herself."

"Mother, I really think my bird is a fairy bird, and all these splendid things come from him," said Tilly, laughing and crying with joy.

It really did seem so, for as she spoke, the robin flew to the table, hopped to the nosegay, and perching among the roses, began to chirp with all his little might. The sun streamed in on flowers, bird, and happy child, and no one saw a shadow glide away from the window; no one ever knew that Mr. King had seen and heard the little girls the night before, or dreamed that the rich neighbor had learned a lesson from the poor neighbor.

And Tilly's bird was a fairy bird; for by her love and tenderness to the helpless thing, she brought good gifts to herself, happiness to the unknown giver of them, and a faithful little friend who did not fly away, but stayed with her till the snow was gone, making summer for her in the winter-time.

Rosa's Tale

"Now, I believe every one has had a Christmas present and a good time. Nobody has been forgotten, not even the cat," said Mrs. Ward to her daughter, as she looked at Pobbylinda, purring on the rug, with a new ribbon round her neck and the remains of a chicken bone between her paws.

It was very late, for the Christmas-tree was stripped, the little folks abed, the baskets and bundles left at poor neighbors' doors, and everything ready for the happy day which would begin as the clock struck twelve. They were resting after their labors, while the yule log burned down; but the mother's words reminded Belinda of one good friend who had received no gift that night.

"We've forgotten Rosa! Her mistress is away, but she shall have a present nevertheless. Late as it is, she will like some apples and cake and a Merry Christmas from the family."

Belinda jumped up as she spoke, and, having collected such remnants of the feast as a horse would relish, she put on her hood, lighted a lantern, and trotted off to the barn.

As she opened the door of the loose box in which Rosa was kept, she saw her eyes shining in the dark as she lifted her head with a startled air. Then, recognizing a friend, she rose and came rustling through the straw to greet her late visitor. She was evidently much pleased with the attention, and rubbed her nose against Miss Belinda gratefully, but seemed rather dainty, and poked over the contents of the basket, as if a little suspicious, though apples were her favorite treat.

Knowing that she would enjoy the little feast more if she had company while she ate it, for Rosa was a very social beast, Miss Belinda hung up the lantern, and, sitting down on an inverted bucket, watched her as she munched contentedly.

"Now really," said Miss Belinda, when telling her story afterwards, "I am not sure whether I took a nap and dreamed what follows, or whether it actually happened, for strange things do occur at Christmas time, as every one knows.

"As I sat there the town clock struck twelve, and the sound reminded me of the legend which affirms that all dumb animals are endowed with speech for one hour after midnight on Christmas eve, in memory of the animals about the manger when the blessed Child was born.

"'I wish the pretty fancy was a fact, and our Rosa could speak, if only for an hour, because I am sure she has an interesting history, and I long to know it.'

"I said this aloud, and to my utter amazement the bay mare stopped eating, fixed her intelligent eyes upon my face, and answered in a language I understood perfectly well,—

"'You shall know it, for whether the legend is true or not I feel as if I could confide in you and tell you all I feel. I was lying awake listening to the fun in the house, thinking of my dear mistress over the sea and feeling very sad, for I heard you say I was to be sold. That nearly broke my heart, for no one has ever been so kind to me as Miss Merry, and nowhere shall I be taken care of, nursed, and loved as I have been since she bought me. I know I am getting old, and stiff in the knees, and my forefoot is lame, and sometimes I'm cross when my shoulder aches; but I do try to be a patient, grateful beast. I've got fat with good living, my work is not hard, I dearly love to carry those who have done so much for me, and I'll tug for them till I die in harness, if they will only keep me.'

"I was so astonished at this address that I tumbled off the pail, and sat among the straw staring up at Rosa, as dumb as if I had lost the power she had gained. She seemed to enjoy my surprise, and added to it by letting me hear a genuine horse laugh, hearty, shrill, and clear, as she shook her pretty head, and went on talking rapidly in the language which I now perceived to be a mixture of English and the peculiar dialect of the horse-country Gulliver visited.

"'Thank you for remembering me to-night, and in return for the goodies you bring I'll tell my story as fast as I can, for I have often longed to recount the trials and triumphs of my life. Miss Merry came last Christmas eve to bring me sugar, and I wanted to speak, but it was too early and I could not say a word, though my heart was full.'

"Rosa paused an instant, and her fine eyes dimmed as if with tender tears at the recollection of the happy year which had followed the day she was bought from the drudgery of a livery-stable to be a lady's pet. I stroked her neck as she stooped to sniff affectionately at my hood, and said eagerly,—

"'Tell away, dear, I'm full of interest, and understand every word you say.'

"Thus encouraged, Rosa threw up her head, and began with an air of pride which plainly proved, what we had always suspected, that she belonged to a good family.

"'My father was a famous racer, and I am very like him; the same color, spirit, and grace, and but for the cruelty of man I might have been as renowned as he. I was a very happy colt, petted by my master, tamed by love, and never struck a blow while he lived. I gained one race for him, and promised so well that when he died I brought a great price. I mourned for him, but was glad to be sent to my new owner's racing-stable and made much of, for people predicted that I should be another Goldsmith Maid or Flora Temple. Ah, how ambitious and proud I was in those days! Vain of my good blood, my speed, and my beauty; for indeed I was handsome then, though you may find it hard to believe now.' And Rosa sighed regretfully as she stole a look at me, and took the attitude which showed to advantage the fine lines about her head and neck.

"'I do not find it hard, for we have always said you had splendid points about you. Miss Merry saw them, though you were a skeleton, when she bought you; so did the skilful Cornish blacksmith when he shod you. And it is easy to see that you belong to a good family by the way you hold your head without a check-rein and carry your tail like a plume,' I said, with a look of admiration which comforted her as much as if she had been a passée belle.

"'I must hurry over this part of my story, because, though brilliant, it was very brief, and ended in a way which made it the bitterest portion of my life,' continued Rosa. 'I won several races, and great fame was predicted for me. You may guess how high my reputation was when I tell you that before my last fatal trial thousands were bet on me, and my rival trembled in his shoes. I was full of spirit, eager to show my speed and sure of success. Alas, how little I knew of the wickedness of human nature then, how dearly I bought the knowledge, and how it has changed my whole life! You do not know much about such matters, of course, and I won't digress to tell you all the tricks of the trade; only beware of jockeys and never bet.

"'I was kept carefully out of every one's way for weeks, and only taken out for exercise by my trainer. Poor Bill! I was fond of him, and he was so good to me that I never have forgotten him, though he broke his neck years ago. A few nights before the great race, as I was getting a good sleep, carefully tucked away in my roomy stall, some one stole in and gave me a warm mash. It was dark, I was half awake, and I ate it like a fool, though I knew by instinct that it was not Bill who fed it to me. I was a confiding creature then, and as all sorts of queer things had been done to prepare me I thought it was all right. But it was not, and that deceit has caused me to be suspicious about my food ever since, for the mash was dosed in some way; it made me very ill, and my enemies nearly triumphed, thanks to this cowardly trick.

"'Bill worked over me day and night, that I might be fit to run. I did my best to seem well and gay, but there was not time for me to regain my lost strength and spirit, and pride alone kept me up. "I'll win for my master if I die in doing it," I said to myself, and when the hour came pranced to my place trying to look as well as ever, though my heart was very heavy and I trembled with excitement.

"Courage, my lass, and we'll beat in spite of their black tricks," whispered Bill, as he sprung to his place.

"'I lost the first heat, but won the second, and the sound of the cheering gave me strength to walk away without staggering, though my legs shook under me. What a splendid minute that was when, encouraged and refreshed by my faithful Bill, I came on the track again! I knew my enemies began to fear, for I had borne myself so bravely they fancied I was quite well, and now, excited by that first success, I was mad with impatience to be off and cover myself with glory.'

"Rosa looked as if the 'splendid minute' had come again, for she arched her neck, opened wide her red nostrils, and pawed the straw with one little foot, while her eyes shone with sudden fire, and her ears were pricked up as if to catch again the shouts she heard that day.

"'I wish I had been there to see you!' I exclaimed, quite carried away by her ardor.

"'I wish you had, for I won, I won! The big black horse did his best, but I had vowed to win or die, and I kept my word, for I beat him by a head, and then dropped as if dead. I might as well have died then, people thought, for the poison, the exertion, and the fall ruined me for a racer. My master cared no more for me, and would have had me shot if Bill had not saved my life. I was pronounced good for nothing, and he bought me cheap. I was lame and useless for a long time, but his patient care did wonders, and just as I was able to be of use to him he was killed.

"'A gentleman in want of a saddle-horse purchased me because my easy gait and quiet temper suited him; for I was meek enough now, and my size fitted me to carry his delicate daughter.

"'For more than a year I served little Miss Alice, rejoicing to see how rosy her pale cheeks became, how upright her feeble figure grew, thanks to the hours spent with me; for my canter rocked her as gently as if she were in a cradle, and fresh air was the medicine she needed. She often said she owed her life to me, and I liked to think so, for she made my life a very easy one.

"'But somehow my good times never lasted long, and when Miss Alice went West I was sold. I had been so well treated that I looked as handsome and gay as ever, though my shoulder never was strong again, and I often had despondent moods, longing for the excitement of the race-course with the instinct of my kind; so I was glad when, attracted by my spirit and beauty, a young army officer bought me and I went to the war. Ah! you never guessed that, did you? Yes, I did my part gallantly and saved my master's life more than once. You have observed how martial music delights me, but you don't know that it is because it reminds me of the proudest hour of my life. I've told you about the saddest; let me relate this also, and give me a pat for the brave action which won my master his promotion, though I got no praise for my part of the achievement.

"'In one of the hottest battles my captain was ordered to lead his men to a most perilous exploit. They hesitated, so did he; for it must cost many lives, and, brave as they were, they paused an instant. But I settled the point, for I was wild with the sound of drums, the smell of powder, the excitement of the hour, and, finding myself sharply reined in, I rebelled, took the bit between my teeth, and dashed straight away into the midst of the fight, spite of all my rider could do. The men thought their captain led them on, and with a cheer they followed, carrying all before them.

"'What happened just after that I never could remember, except that I got a wound here in my neck and a cut on my flank; the scar is there still, and I'm proud of it, though buyers always consider it a blemish. But when the battle was won my master was promoted on the field, and I carried him up to the general as he sat among his officers under the torn flags.

"'Both of us were weary and wounded, both were full of pride at what we had done; but he got all the praise and the honor, I only a careless word and a better supper than usual.

"'I thought no one knew what I had done, and resented the ingratitude of your race; for it was the horse, not the man, who led that forlorn hope, and I did think I should have a rosette at least, when others got stars and bars for far less dangerous deeds. Never mind, my master knew the truth, and thanked me for my help by keeping me always with him till the sad day when he was shot in a skirmish, and lay for hours with none to watch and mourn over him but his faithful horse.

"'Then I knew how much he loved and thanked me, for his hand stroked me while it had the strength, his eye turned to me till it grew too dim for seeing, and when help came, among the last words he whispered to a comrade were these, "Be kind to Rosa and send her safely home; she has earned her rest."

"'I had earned it, but I did not get it, for when I was sent home the old mother's heart was broken at the loss of her son, and she did not live long to cherish me. Then my hard times began, for my next owner was a fast young man, who ill used me in many ways, till the spirit of my father rose within me, and I gave my brutal master a grand runaway and smash-up.

"'To tame me down, I was sold for a car horse; and that almost killed me, for it was dreadful drudgery to tug, day after day, over the hard pavement with heavy loads behind me, uncongenial companions beside me, and no affection to cheer my life.

"'I have often longed to ask why Mr. Bergh does not try to prevent such crowds from piling into those cars; and now I beg you to do what you can to stop such an unmerciful abuse.

"'In snow-storms it was awful, and more than one of my mates dropped dead with overwork and discouragement. I used to wish I could do the same, for my poor feet, badly shod, became so lame I could hardly walk at times, and the constant strain on the up grades brought back the old trouble in my shoulder worse than ever.

"'Why they did not kill me I don't know, for I was a miserable creature then; but there must be something attractive about me, I fancy, for people always seem to think me worth saving. What can it be, ma'am?'

"'Now, Rosa, don't be affected; you know you are a very engaging little animal, and if you live to be forty will still have certain pretty ways about you, that win the hearts of women, if not of men. They see your weak points, and take a money view of the case; but we sympathize with your afflictions, are amused with your coquettish airs, and like your affectionate nature. Now hurry up and finish, for I find it a trifle cold out here.'

"I laughed as I spoke, for Rosa eyed me with a sidelong glance and gently waved the docked tail, which was her delight; for the sly thing liked to be flattered and was as fond of compliments as a girl.

"'Many thanks. I will come now to the most interesting portion of my narrative. As I was saying, instead of knocking me on the head I was packed off to New Hampshire, and had a fine rest among the green hills, with a dozen or so of weary friends. It was during this holiday that I acquired the love of nature which Miss Merry detected and liked in me, when she found me ready to study sunsets with her, to admire new landscapes, and enjoy bright summer weather.

"'In the autumn a livery-stable keeper bought me, and through the winter fed me up till I was quite presentable in the spring. It was a small town, but through the summer many city people visited there, so I was kept on the trot while the season lasted, because ladies could drive me. You, Miss Belinda, were one of the ladies, and I never shall forget, though I have long ago forgiven it, how you laughed at my queer gait the day you hired me.

"'My tender feet and stiff knees made me tread very gingerly, and amble along with short mincing steps, which contrasted oddly, I know, with my proudly waving tail and high-carried head. You liked me nevertheless, because I didn't rattle you down the steep hills, was not afraid of locomotives, and stood patiently while you gathered flowers and enjoyed the lovely prospects.

"'I have always felt a regard for you since you did not whip me, and admired my eyes, which, I may say without vanity, have always been considered unusually fine. But no one ever won my whole heart like Miss Merry, and I never shall forget the happy day when she came to the stable to order a saddle-horse. Her cheery voice made me prick up my ears, and when she said, after looking at several showy beasts, "No, they don't suit me. This one now has the right air; can I ride her?" my heart danced within me and I looked round with a whinny of delight. She understood my welcome, and came right up to me, patted me, peered into my face, rubbed my nose, and looked at my feet with an air of interest and sympathy, that made me feel as if I'd like to carry her round the world.

"'Ah, what rides we had after that! What happy hours trotting gayly through the green woods, galloping over the breezy hills, or pacing slowly along quiet lanes, where I often lunched luxuriously on clover-tops, while Miss Merry took a sketch of some picturesque bit with me in the foreground.

"'I liked that, and we had long chats at such times, for she seemed to understand me perfectly. She was never frightened when I danced for pleasure on the soft turf, never chid me when I snatched a bite from the young trees as we passed through sylvan ways, never thought it a trouble to let me wet my tired feet in babbling brooks, or to dismount and take out the stones that plagued me.

"'Then how well she rode! So firm yet light a seat, so steady a hand, so agile a foot to spring on and off, and such infectious spirits, that no matter how despondent or cross I might be, in five minutes I felt gay and young again when dear Miss Merry was on my back.'

"Here Rosa gave a frisk that sent the straw flying, and made me shrink into a corner, while she pranced about the box with a neigh which waked the big brown colt next door, and set poor Buttercup to lowing for her calf, the loss of which she had forgotten for a little while in sleep.

"'Ah, Miss Merry never ran away from me! She knew my heels were to be trusted, and she let me caper as I would, glad to see me lively. Never mind, Miss Belinda, come out and I'll be sober, as befits my years,' laughed Rosa, composing herself, and adding, so like a woman that I could not help smiling in the dark,—

"'When I say "years" I beg you to understand that I am not as old as that base man declared, but just in the prime of life for a horse. Hard usage has made me seem old before my time, and I am good for years of service yet.'

"'Few people have been through as much as you have, Rosa, and you certainly have earned the right to rest,' I said consolingly, for her little whims and vanities amused me much.

"'You know what happened next,' she continued; 'but I must seize this opportunity to express my thanks for all the kindness I've received since Miss Merry bought me, in spite of the ridicule and dissuasion of all her friends.

"'I know I didn't look like a good bargain, for I was very thin and lame and shabby; but she saw and loved the willing spirit in me, pitied my hard lot, and felt that it would be a good deed to buy me even if she never got much work out of me.

"'I shall always remember that, and whatever happens to me hereafter, I never shall be as proud again as I was the day she put my new saddle and bridle on, and I was led out, sleek, plump, and handsome, with blue rosettes at my ears, my tail cut in the English style, and on my back Miss Merry in her London hat and habit, all ready to head a cavalcade of eighteen horsemen and horsewomen. We were the most perfect pair of all, and when the troop caracoled down the wide street six abreast, my head was the highest, my rider the straightest, and our two hearts the friendliest in all the goodly company.

"'Nor is it pride and love alone that binds me to her, it is gratitude as well, for did not she often bathe my feet herself, rub me down, water me, blanket me, and daily come to see me when I was here alone for weeks in the winter time? Didn't she study horses' feet and shoes, that I might be cured if possible? Didn't she write to the famous friend of my race for advice, and drive me seven miles to get a good smith to shoe me well? Have not my poor contracted feet grown much better, thanks to the weeks of rest without shoes which she gave me? Am I not fat and handsome, and, barring the stiff knees, a very presentable horse? If I am, it is all owing to her; and for that reason I want to live and die in her service.

"'She doesn't want to sell me, and only bade you do it because you didn't want the care of me while she is gone. Dear Miss Belinda, please keep me! I'll eat as little as I can. I won't ask for a new blanket, though your old army one is very thin and shabby. I'll trot for you all winter, and try not to show it if I am lame. I'll do anything a horse can, no matter how humble, to earn my living, only don't, pray don't send me away among strangers who have neither interest nor pity for me!'

"Rosa had spoken rapidly, feeling that her plea must be made now or never, for before another Christmas she might be far away and speech of no use to win her wish. I was much touched, though she was only a horse; for she was looking earnestly at me as she spoke, and made the last words very eloquent by preparing to bend her stiff knees and lie down at my feet. I stopped her, and answered, with an arm about her neck and her soft nose in my hand,—

"'You shall not be sold, Rosa! you shall go and board at Mr. Town's great stable, where you will have pleasant society among the eighty horses who usually pass the winter there. Your shoes shall be taken off, and you shall rest till March at least. The best care will be taken of you, dear, and I will come and see you; and in the spring you shall return to us, even if Miss Merry is not here to welcome you.'

"'Thanks, many, many thanks! But I wish I could do something to earn my board. I hate to be idle, though rest is delicious. Is there nothing I can do to repay you, Miss Belinda? Please answer quickly, for I know the hour is almost over,' cried Rosa, stamping with anxiety; for, like all her sex, she wanted the last word.

"'Yes, you can,' I cried, as a sudden idea popped into my head. 'I'll write down what you have told me, and send the little story to a certain paper I know of, and the money I get for it will pay your board. So rest in peace, my dear; you will have earned your living, and may feel that your debt is paid.'

"Before she could reply the clock struck one, and a long sigh of satisfaction was all the response in her power. But we understood each other now, and, cutting a lock from her mane for Miss Merry, I gave Rosa a farewell caress and went away, wondering if I had made it all up, or if she had really broken a year's silence and freed her mind.

"However that may be, here is the tale, and the sequel to it is, that the bay mare has really gone to board at a first-class stable," concluded Miss Belinda. "I call occasionally and leave my card in the shape of an apple, finding Madam Rosa living like an independent lady, with her large box and private yard on the sunny side of the barn, a kind ostler to wait upon her, and much genteel society from the city when she is inclined for company.

"What more could any reasonable horse desire?"

What The Bells Saw And Said

"Bells ring others to church, but go not in themselves."

No one saw the spirits of the bells up there in the old steeple at midnight on Christmas Eve. Six quaint figures, each wrapped in a shadowy cloak and wearing a bell-shaped cap. All were gray-headed, for they were among the oldest bell-spirits of the city, and "the light of other days" shone in their thoughtful eyes. Silently they sat, looking down on the snow-covered roofs glittering in the moonlight, and the quiet streets deserted by all but the watchmen on their chilly rounds, and such poor souls as wandered shelterless in the winter night. Presently one of the spirits said, in a tone, which, low as it was, filled the belfry with reverberating echoes,

"Well, brothers, are your reports ready of the year that now lies dying?"

All bowed their heads, and one of the oldest answered in a sonorous voice:

"My report isn't all I could wish. You know I look down on the commercial part of our city and have fine opportunities for seeing what goes on there. It's my business to watch the business men, and upon my word I'm heartily ashamed of them sometimes. During the war they did nobly, giving their time and money, their sons and selves to the good cause, and I was proud of them. But now too many of them have fallen back into the old ways, and their motto seems to be, 'Every one for himself, and the devil take the hindmost.' Cheating, lying and stealing are hard words, and I don't mean to apply them to all who swarm about below there like ants on an ant-hill, they have other names for these things, but I'm old-fashioned and use plain words. There's a deal too much dishonesty in the world, and business seems to have become a game of hazard in which luck, not labor, wins the prize. When I was young, men were years making moderate fortunes, and were satisfied with them. They built them on sure foundations, knew how to enjoy them while they lived, and to leave a good name behind them when they died.

"Now it's anything for money; health, happiness, honor, life itself, are flung down on that great gaming-table, and they forget everything else in the excitement of success or the desperation of defeat. Nobody seems satisfied either, for those who win have little time or taste to enjoy their prosperity, and those who lose have little courage or patience to support them in adversity. They don't even fail as they used to. In my day when a merchant found himself embarrassed he didn't ruin others in order to save himself, but honestly confessed the truth, gave up everything, and began again. But now-a-days after all manner of dishonorable shifts there comes a grand crash; many suffer, but by some hocus-pocus the merchant saves enough to retire upon and live comfortably here or abroad. It's very evident that honor and honesty don't mean now what they used to mean in the days of old May, Higginson and Lawrence.

"They preach below here, and very well too sometimes, for I often slide down the rope to peep and listen during service. But, bless you! they don't seem to lay either sermon, psalm or prayer to heart, for while the minister is doing his best, the congregation, tired with the breathless hurry of the week, sleep peacefully, calculate their chances for the morrow, or wonder which of their neighbors will lose or win in the great game. Don't tell me! I've seen them do it, and if I dared I'd have startled every soul of them with a rousing peal. Ah, they don't dream whose eye is on them, they never guess what secrets the telegraph wires tell as the messages fly by, and little know what a report I give to the winds of heaven as I ring out above them morning, noon, and night." And the old spirit shook his head till the tassel on his cap jangled like a little bell.

"There are some, however, whom I love and honor," he said, in a benignant tone, "who honestly earn their bread, who deserve all the success that comes to them, and always keep a warm corner in their noble hearts for those less blest than they. These are the men who serve the city in times of peace, save it in times of war, deserve the highest honors in its gift, and leave behind them a record that keeps their memories green. For such an one we lately tolled a knell, my brothers; and as our united voices pealed over the city, in all grateful hearts, sweeter and more solemn than any chime, rung the words that made him so beloved,

"'Treat our dead boys tenderly, and send them home to me.'"

He ceased, and all the spirits reverently uncovered their gray heads as a strain of music floated up from the sleeping city and died among the stars.

"Like yours, my report is not satisfactory in all respects," began the second spirit, who wore a very pointed cap and a finely ornamented cloak. But, though his dress was fresh and youthful, his face was old, and he had nodded several times during his brother's speech. "My greatest affliction during the past year has been the terrible extravagance which prevails. My post, as you know, is at the court end of the city, and I see all the fashionable vices and follies. It is a marvel to me how so many of these immortal creatures, with such opportunities for usefulness, self-improvement and genuine happiness can be content to go round and round in one narrow circle of unprofitable and unsatisfactory pursuits. I do my best to warn them; Sunday after Sunday I chime in their ears the beautiful old hymns that sweetly chide or cheer the hearts that truly listen and believe; Sunday after Sunday I look down on them as they pass in, hoping to see that my words have not fallen upon deaf ears; and Sunday after Sunday they listen to words that should teach them much, yet seem to go by them like the wind. They are told to love their neighbor, yet too many hate him because he possesses more of this world's goods or honors than they: they are told that a rich man cannot enter the kingdom of heaven, yet they go on laying up perishable wealth, and though often warned that moth and rust will corrupt, they fail to believe it till the worm that destroys enters and mars their own chapel of ease. Being a spirit, I see below external splendor and find much poverty of heart and soul under the velvet and the ermine which should cover rich and royal natures. Our city saints walk abroad in threadbare suits, and under quiet bonnets shine the eyes that make sunshine in the shady places. Often as I watch the glittering procession passing to and fro below me. I wonder if, with all our progress, there is to-day as much real piety as in the times when our fathers, poorly clad, with weapon in one hand and Bible in the other, came weary distances to worship in the wilderness with fervent faith unquenched by danger, suffering and solitude.

"Yet in spite of my fault-finding I love my children, as I call them, for all are not butterflies. Many find wealth no temptation to forgetfulness of duty or hardness of heart. Many give freely of their abundance, pity the poor, comfort the afflicted, and make our city loved and honored in other lands as in our own. They have their cares, losses, and heartaches as well as the poor; it isn't all sunshine with them, and they learn, poor souls, that

"'Into each life some rain must fall,
Some days must be dark and dreary.'

"But I've hopes of them, and lately they have had a teacher so genial, so gifted, so well-beloved that all who listen to him must be better for the lessons of charity, good-will and cheerfulness which he brings home to them by the magic of tears and smiles. We know him, we love him, we always remember him as the year comes round, and the blithest song our brazen tongues utter is a Christmas carol to the Father of 'The Chimes!'"

As the spirit spoke his voice grew cheery, his old face shone, and in a burst of hearty enthusiasm he flung up his cap and cheered like a boy. So did the others, and as the fairy shout echoed through the belfry a troop of shadowy figures, with faces lovely or grotesque, tragical or gay, sailed by on the wings of the wintry wind and waved their hands to the spirits of the bells.

As the excitement subsided and the spirits reseated themselves, looking ten years younger for that burst, another spoke. A venerable brother in a dingy mantle, with a tuneful voice, and eyes that seemed to have grown sad with looking on much misery.

"He loves the poor, the man we've just hurrahed for, and he makes others love and remember them, bless him!" said the spirit. "I hope he'll touch the hearts of those who listen to him here and beguile them to open their hands to my unhappy children over yonder. If I could set some of the forlorn souls in my parish beside the happier creatures who weep over imaginary woes as they are painted by his eloquent lips, that brilliant scene would be better than any sermon. Day and night I look down on lives as full of sin, self-sacrifice and suffering as any in those famous books. Day and night I try to comfort the poor by my cheery voice, and to make their wants known by proclaiming them with all my might. But people seem to be so intent on business, pleasure or home duties that they have no time to hear and answer my appeal. There's a deal of charity in this good city, and when the people do wake up they work with a will; but I can't help thinking that if some of the money lavished on luxuries was spent on necessaries for the poor, there would be fewer tragedies like that which ended yesterday. It's a short story, easy to tell, though long and hard to live; listen to it.

"Down yonder in the garret of one of the squalid houses at the foot of my tower, a little girl has lived for a year, fighting silently and single-handed a good fight against poverty and sin. I saw her when she first came, a hopeful, cheerful, brave-hearted little soul, alone, yet not afraid. She used to sit all day sewing at her window, and her lamp burnt far into the night, for she was very poor, and all she earned would barely give her food and shelter. I watched her feed the doves, who seemed to be her only friends; she never forgot them, and daily gave them the few crumbs that fell from her meagre table. But there was no kind hand to feed and foster the little human dove, and so she starved.

"For a while she worked bravely, but the poor three dollars a week would not clothe and feed and warm her, though the things her busy fingers made sold for enough to keep her comfortably if she had received it. I saw the pretty color fade from her cheeks; her eyes grew hollow, her voice lost its cheery ring, her step its elasticity, and her face began to wear the haggard, anxious look that made its youth doubly pathetic. Her poor little gowns grew shabby, her shawl so thin she shivered when the pitiless wind smote her, and her feet were almost bare. Rain and snow beat on the patient little figure going to and fro, each morning with hope and courage faintly shining, each evening with the shadow of despair gathering darker round her. It was a hard time for all, desperately hard for her, and in her poverty, sin and pleasure tempted her. She resisted, but as another bitter winter came she feared that in her misery she might yield, for body and soul were weakened now by the long struggle. She knew not where to turn for help; there seemed to be no place for her at any safe and happy fireside; life's hard aspect daunted her, and she turned to death, saying confidingly, 'Take me while I'm innocent and not afraid to go.'

"I saw it all! I saw how she sold everything that would bring money and paid her little debts to the utmost penny; how she set her poor room in order for the last time; how she tenderly bade the doves good-by, and lay down on her bed to die. At nine o'clock last night as my bell rang over the city, I tried to tell what was going on in the garret where the light was dying out so fast. I cried to them with all my strength.

"'Kind souls, below there! a fellow-creature is perishing for lack of charity! Oh, help her before it is too late! Mothers, with little daughters on your knees, stretch out your hands and take her in! Happy women, in the safe shelter of home, think of her desolation! Rich men, who grind the faces of the poor, remember that this soul will one day be required of you! Dear Lord, let not this little sparrow fall to the ground! Help, Christian men and women, in the name of Him whose birthday blessed the world!'

"Ah me! I rang, and clashed, and cried in vain. The passers-by only said, as they hurried home, laden with Christmas cheer: 'The old bell is merry to-night, as it should be at this blithe season, bless it!'

"As the clocks struck ten, the poor child lay down, saying, as she drank the last bitter draught life could give her, 'It's very cold, but soon I shall not feel it;' and with her quiet eyes fixed on the cross that glimmered in the moonlight above me, she lay waiting for the sleep that needs no lullaby.

"As the clock struck eleven, pain and poverty for her were over. It was bitter cold, but she no longer felt it. She lay serenely sleeping, with tired heart and hands, at rest forever. As the clocks struck twelve, the dear Lord remembered her, and with fatherly hand led her into the home where there is room for all. To-day I rung her knell, and though my heart was heavy, yet my soul was glad; for in spite of all her human woe and weakness, I am sure that little girl will keep a joyful Christmas up in heaven."

In the silence which the spirits for a moment kept, a breath of softer air than any from the snowy world below swept through the steeple and seemed to whisper, "Yes!"

"Avast there! fond as I am of salt water, I don't like this kind," cried the breezy voice of the fourth spirit, who had a tiny ship instead of a tassel on his cap, and who wiped his wet eyes with the sleeve of his rough blue cloak. "It won't take me long to spin my yarn; for things are pretty taut and ship-shape aboard our craft. Captain Taylor is an experienced sailor, and has brought many a ship safely into port in spite of wind and tide, and the devil's own whirlpools and hurricanes. If you want to see earnestness come aboard some Sunday when the Captain's on the quarter-deck, and take an observation. No danger of falling asleep there, no more than there is up aloft, 'when the stormy winds do blow.' Consciences get raked fore and aft, sins are blown clean out of the water, false colors are hauled down and true ones run up to the masthead, and many an immortal soul is warned to steer off in time from the pirates, rocks and quicksands of temptation. He's a regular revolving light, is the Captain, a beacon always burning and saying plainly, 'Here are life-boats, ready to put off in all weathers and bring the shipwrecked into quiet waters.' He comes but seldom now, being laid up in the home dock, tranquilly waiting till his turn comes to go out with the tide and safely ride at anchor in the great harbor of the Lord. Our crew varies a good deal. Some of 'em have rather rough voyages, and come into port pretty well battered; land-sharks fall foul of a good many, and do a deal of damage; but most of 'em carry brave and tender hearts under the blue jackets, for their rough nurse, the sea, manages to keep something of the child alive in the grayest old tar that makes the world his picture-book. We try to supply 'em with life-preservers while at sea, and make 'em feel sure of a hearty welcome when ashore, and I believe the year '67 will sail away into eternity with a satisfactory cargo. Brother North-End made me pipe my eye; so I'll make him laugh to pay for it, by telling a clerical joke I heard the other day. Bellows didn't make it, though he might have done so, as he's a connection of ours, and knows how to use his tongue as well as any of us. Speaking of the bells of a certain town, a reverend gentleman affirmed that each bell uttered an appropriate remark so plainly, that the words were audible to all. The Baptist bell cried, briskly, 'Come up and be dipped! come up and be dipped!' The Episcopal bell slowly said, 'Apos-tol-ic suc-cess-ion! apos-tol-ic suc-cess-ion!' The Orthodox bell solemnly pronounced, 'Eternal damnation! eternal damnation!' and the Methodist shouted, invitingly, 'Room for all! room for all!'"

As the spirit imitated the various calls, as only a jovial bell-sprite could, the others gave him a chime of laughter, and vowed they would each adopt some tuneful summons, which should reach human ears and draw human feet more willingly to church.

"Faith, brother, you've kept your word and got the laugh out of us," cried a stout, sleek spirit, with a kindly face, and a row of little saints round his cap and a rosary at his side. "It's very well we are doing this year; the cathedral is full, the flock increasing, and the true faith holding its own entirely. Ye may shake your heads if you will and fear there'll be trouble, but I doubt it. We've warm hearts of our own, and the best of us don't forget that when we were starving, America, the saints bless the jewel! sent us bread; when we were dying for lack of work, America opened her arms and took us in, and now helps us to build churches, homes and schools by giving us a share of the riches all men work for and win. It's a generous nation ye are, and a brave one, and we showed our gratitude by fighting for ye in the day of trouble and giving ye our Phil, and many another broth of a boy. The land is wide enough for us both, and while we work and fight and grow together, each may learn something from the other. I'm free to confess that your religion looks a bit cold and hard to me, even here in the good city where each man may ride his own hobby to death, and hoot at his neighbors as much as he will. You seem to keep your piety shut up all the week in your bare, white churches, and only let it out on Sundays, just a trifle musty with disuse. You set your rich, warm and soft to the fore, and leave the poor shivering at the door. You give your people bare walls to look upon, common-place music to listen to, dull sermons to put them asleep, and then wonder why they stay away, or take no interest when they come.

"We leave our doors open day and night; our lamps are always burning, and we may come into our Father's house at any hour. We let rich and poor kneel together, all being equal there. With us abroad you'll see prince and peasant side by side, school-boy and bishop, market-woman and noble lady, saint and sinner, praying to the Holy Mary, whose motherly arms are open to high and low. We make our churches inviting with immortal music, pictures by the world's great masters, and rites that are splendid symbols of the faith we hold. Call it mummery if ye like, but let me ask you why so many of your sheep stray into our fold? It's because they miss the warmth, the hearty, the maternal tenderness which all souls love and long for, and fail to find in your stern. Puritanical belief. By Saint Peter! I've seen many a lukewarm worshipper, who for years has nodded in your cushioned pews, wake and glow with something akin to genuine piety while kneeling on the stone pavement of one of our cathedrals, with Raphael's angels before his eyes, with strains of magnificent music in his ears, and all about him, in shapes of power or beauty, the saints and martyrs who have saved the world, and whose presence inspires him to follow their divine example. It's not complaining of ye I am, but just reminding ye that men are but children after all, and need more tempting to virtue than they do to vice, which last comes easy to 'em since the Fall. Do your best in your own ways to get the poor souls into bliss, and good luck to ye. But remember, there's room in the Holy Mother Church for all, and when your own priests send ye to the divil, come straight to us and we'll take ye in."

"A truly Catholic welcome, bull and all," said the sixth spirit, who, in spite of his old-fashioned garments, had a youthful face, earnest, fearless eyes, and an energetic voice that woke the echoes with its vigorous tones. "I've a hopeful report, brothers, for the reforms of the day are wheeling into rank and marching on. The war isn't over nor rebeldom conquered yet, but the Old Guard has been 'up and at 'em' through the year. There has been some hard fighting, rivers of ink have flowed, and the Washington dawdlers have signalized themselves by a 'masterly inactivity.' The political campaign has been an anxious one; some of the leaders have deserted; some been mustered out; some have fallen gallantly, and as yet have received no monuments. But at the Grand Review the Cross of the Legion of Honor will surely shine on many a brave breast that won no decoration but its virtue here; for the world's fanatics make heaven's heroes, poets say.

"The flock of Nightingales that flew South during the 'winter of our discontent' are all at home again, some here and some in Heaven. But the music of their womanly heroism still lingers in the nation's memory, and makes a tender minor-chord in the battle-hymn of freedom.

"The reform in literature isn't as vigorous as I could wish; but a sharp attack of mental and moral dyspepsia will soon teach our people that French confectionery and the bad pastry of Wood, Bracdon, Yates & Co. is not the best diet for the rising generation.

"Speaking of the rising generation reminds me of the schools. They are doing well; they always are, and we are justly proud of them. There may be a slight tendency toward placing too much value upon book-learning; too little upon home culture. Our girls are acknowledged to be uncommonly pretty, witty and wise, but some of us wish they had more health and less excitement, more domestic accomplishments and fewer ologies and isms, and were contented with simple pleasures and the old-fashioned virtues, and not quite so fond of the fast, frivolous life that makes them old so soon. I am fond of our girls and boys. I love to ring for their christenings and marriages, to toll proudly for the brave lads in blue, and tenderly for the innocent creatures whose seats are empty under my old roof. I want to see them anxious to make Young America a model of virtue, strength and beauty, and I believe they will in time.

"There have been some important revivals in religion; for the world won't stand still, and we must keep pace or be left behind to fossilize. A free nation must have a religion broad enough to embrace all mankind, deep enough to fathom and fill the human soul, high enough to reach the source of all love and wisdom, and pure enough to satisfy the wisest and the best. Alarm bells have been rung, anathemas pronounced, and Christians, forgetful of their creed, have abused one another heartily. But the truth always triumphs in the end, and whoever sincerely believes, works and waits for it, by whatever name he calls it, will surely find his own faith blessed to him in proportion to his charity for the faith of others.

"But look! the first red streaks of dawn are in the East. Our vigil is over, and we must fly home to welcome in the holidays. Before we part, join with me, brothers, in resolving that through the coming year we will with all our hearts and tongues,

"'Ring out the old, ring in the new,
Ring out the false, ring in the true;
Ring in the valiant man and free,
Ring in the Christ that is to be.'"

Then hand in hand the spirits of the bells floated away, singing in the hush of dawn the sweet song the stars sung over Bethlehem, "Peace on earth, good will to men."

A Song For A Christmas Tree
Cold and wintry is the sky,
Bitter winds go whistling by,
Orchard boughs are bare and dry,
Yet here stands a faithful tree.
Household fairies kind and dear,
With loving magic none need fear,

Bade it rise and blossom here,
Little friends, for you and me.

Come and gather as they fall,
Shining gifts for great and small;
Santa Claus remembers all
When he comes with goodies piled.
Corn and candy, apples red,
Sugar horses, gingerbread,
Babies who are never fed,
Are handing here for every child.

Shake the boughs and down they come,
Better fruit than peach or plum,
'T is our little harvest home;
For though frosts the flowers kill,
Though birds depart and squirrels sleep,
Though snows may gather cold and deep,
Little folks their sunshine keep,
And mother-love makes summer still.

Gathered in a smiling ring,
Lightly dance and gayly sing,
Still at heart remembering
The sweet story all should know,
Of the little Child whose birth
Has made this day throughout the earth
A festival for childish mirth,
Since the first Christmas long ago.

Printed in Great Britain
by Amazon